FIRST MEXICAN

First Mexican

Vio Celaya

iUniverse, Inc.
New York Lincoln Shanghai

First Mexican

iUniverse books may be ordered through booksellers or by contacting:

iUniverse
2021 Pine Lake Road, Suite 100
Lincoln, NE 68512
www.iuniverse.com
1-800-Authors (1-800-288-4677)

This interpretation of politics and government is a figment of my own imagination and the same is true of the names and the characters in this book. Any similarity to actual individuals is pure coincidence.

ISBN-13: 978-0-595-36758-0 (pbk)
ISBN-13: 978-0-595-81177-9 (ebk)
ISBN-10: 0-595-36758-5 (pbk)
ISBN-10: 0-595-81177-9 (ebk)

Printed in the United States of America

I dedicate this book to my beloved wife, Stella, who first encouraged me to write a book. Her support was constant until the day she passed away.

CHAPTER 1

▼

George was exhausted but he kept on running. The sound of his heavy breathing roared in his ears. The hot sweat that poured from his body defied the cold night. His eyes darted back and forth over his shoulders, as he desperately tried to catch a glimpse of who or *what* was chasing him. He tried to see through the thick fog but it was impossible. Even the moonlight could not penetrate the dark gray mist. Suddenly the sound of leather scraping on the wet cobblestone was upon him.

Why was he running? What was the danger that lurked in the darkness? Anxiously he looked for someone to help him. His eyes burned and he could only make out images of unrecognizable shadows floating through the air.

Then he remembered his father's words. *When in danger do not run. Face it; then act according to the threat.*

George decided to stop. He turned and leaned against a cold brick wall that felt wet to the touch. Fatigued, he struggled to stay on his feet as the sidewalk beneath him swayed from side to side. When he caught his breath, he saw a dark figure rapidly walking towards him. Just as George began to shout, he saw the flash of a gun as a shot rang out. Whoever it was turned around and disappeared in the fog.

George felt no pain but he could not breathe. He began to slide down. He put both hands back against the wall but he could not stop sliding. A feeling of helplessness overcame him as he looked down to see why his feet were not there. In horror, he saw his body and clothing melt like ice cubes on a hot plate, as he transformed into a thick liquid gray matter.

He tried to shout out but could not utter a sound. His vocal cords were para-lyzed. It didn't matter anyway; he was beyond help. In an instant, he was gone. In the eerie silence that ensued, the gray liquid ran down the curb onto the asphalt as everything went black.

Suddenly, George jolted straight up in his bed, covered with sweat and wide-awake. As his heart pounded loudly in his chest, he knew he just had another nightmare. It was the third time this year. All three were similar except for the ending. *What does it all mean? Are the nightmares trying to tell me something?* He sat on the bed for a long time trying to come up with an answer. He was drained of energy. *To Hell with it.* Regardless of what the dreams meant, he decided to keep them to himself.

✳   ✳   ✳   ✳

George's mother was dying of cancer. In 1944, a cure for her cancer did not exist. As the youngest child in a family of nine siblings, George did not under-stand what was happening to his beloved mother. The doctor told the family his mother did not have long to live.

In accordance with family tradition, the siblings prepared to see their mother, one at a time, for the last time. The oldest went in first, all the way down to the youngest. She talked to each one alone. George was the last one to go in.

The room was dark except for a small lamp in the far corner, and a dim light glowed from the street lamp outside. Even at his young age, George remembered how odd the light from 23rd Street looked as it hit the crucifix above his mother's bed. The crucifix glowed, as if the light came from the crucifix itself, instead of a reflection from the street lamp. The same light coming through the window also directly hit a picture frame with the American flag, and the image fascinated George. On the opposite wall of the small room, the flag reflected in a mirror to a size larger than George did.

His mother sensed his presence, and softly called to him. "Come here, George. There are some things I want to tell you." George sat on the side of her bed, and they embraced for a long time. George's mother hid her tears as she spoke. "I will be leaving soon, George. There are so many things to say to you, but the time is short. I love you very much."

Silence filled the room, then George whispered, "I love you, Mom, and you don't have to go anywhere." The door opened, and his father walked in and held George's hand as he talked to his mother. His mother died as they all embraced. George would never forget that night as long as he lived.

That same night, George dreamt of the lights in his mother's bedroom. This time, a pale blue light shined on his mother's face. Suddenly, the light grew bigger and brighter. The bluish light fell all around his mother, who wore a beautiful white dress. She stood near his bed and said, "I am leaving now, George. I'll always be near you. You will grow up to be a very famous man some day. There will be many roads in your life but you will always know the right one to take. When you see this light again, it will be at the end of one of these roads. Then we will meet again. Goodbye, George, and God bless you." George woke up crying, and did not sleep the rest of the night.

The Clarkston cemetery was centrally located within a residential neighborhood in the older part of town, but the view was obscured by overgrown and neglected desert vegetation. The day of the funeral was a typically hot and bone-dry day in the Southern Arizona desert. A large contingent of family gathered to pay their last respects. George's father stood in front as if to convey he was in charge. At five foot ten, with green eyes and sandy gray hair, Henry Ramos made an impressive figure. He was a humble man, yet he walked with the stride of a stallion. The blood of Conquistador and Toltec Indian ran through his veins, giving him an aura of nobility.

As the casket slowly disappeared into its final resting place, family members began to sob. George looked up, and in the distance, he saw the mountain with a huge cross at the very top. A tall flagpole towered over the cemetery, and George watched the flag fly in the shadow of the mountain, just a few miles away. He remembered the night in his mother's bedroom and the dream he had. He felt his heart pound, and looked down at his mother's casket for the last time and told her, "Yes, Mother, someday I will be very famous. I will be President of the United States. I promise you."

＊   ＊   ＊   ＊

George's father, Henry, was a Mine Engineer for the New Castle Branch of the Southern Arizona Copper Company, which everyone referred to as "the Company." Fluent in Spanish, Henry worked for "the Company" for over ten years at their open pit copper mining operation in Mexico, ninety-five miles south of the United States border. Mexican law had required him to maintain a residence in Mexico in order to work there.

In the summer of 1945, Southern Arizona Copper Company lost its contractual agreement with the Mexican Government to continue mining operations in

Mexico after a dispute on royalty payments. Henry was forced to transfer to the Clarkston mine and uproot his family to the United States.

The family's move back to Clarkston meant the acceptance of substandard housing for Henry and his remaining five children still living at home. Clarkston was divided into three distinct housing sections. Whites lived in the section of town with chain link fences and concrete sidewalks known as Parkdale. Mexicans were limited to the older section of town simply known as the "Mexican Town." On the outskirts of town, well secluded in a valley of desert vegetation and surrounded by small hills was a settlement of small white wooden dwellings known as the "Indian Village."

Henry had mixed feelings about moving his family to Arizona. On one hand, he was proud to be one of the few Mexican Americans that had a college education and a decent paying job. On the other hand, he was saddened that his children were going to be exposed to the open prejudice towards Mexicans and Native Americans. Mexicans and American Indians were considered second-class citizens in many areas of the Southwest. One of the most notorious practices of discrimination was the limited use of public facilities to Mexicans and American Indians.

Clarkston had one public swimming pool. The swimming pool was open six days a week. On Tuesdays the City workers drained and cleaned the pool water. On Wednesday through Sunday no Mexicans could swim in the pool—only Whites. Mexicans were only allowed to swim on "Mexican Day" which was Monday—the day the water was at its filthiest. This practice continued throughout Southwest until the mid 1950's when a landmark court case forced communities to discontinue discrimination of public facilities against minorities.

The local theater in Clarkston even had a section near the rear, close to the projectionist, that was clearly marked "Mexicans Only." For many Mexicans living in Clarkston these acts of humiliation were a small price to pay for the opportunity to live in the great land of America, and most Mexicans never complained.

Even Henry, a college educated engineer, would have to go through the daily ritual of showering in the "Mexicans Only" shower facility at the mine. The mines in Arizona also notoriously practiced a dual wage system by which Mexicans were paid a lower wage than Whites for the same work done. Henry had to quietly accept that his salary would be less than his white counterparts at the mine. If he complained, he knew he would surely be fired. This practice continued even into 1960's.

After the death of their mother, the older of the two sisters stayed home to do the cooking and other household chores, and to take care of the younger children. The remaining children would now have to attend school in the United States, and Henry was not happy about that.

In the early Forties, many schools in Southern states still practiced segregation. The schools in Clarkston did not have segregated classes, at least not on paper. Curry Elementary School provided three classrooms for each grade level from first to six grades: one classroom for white kids, one for Mexican-Americans, and one for Indian kids. There were no black families in Clarkston. They claimed to do away with segregation by sprinkling a few Mexican-American and Indian kids in the all-white classrooms. A closer examination showed that of the minority students that were sprinkled in, they just happened to all be children of some of the highest paid mine employees. The children of railroad track laborers or janitors never found their way into the all-white classrooms. Henry hoped the children would notice none of this.

*   *   *   *

It was late August and the first day of registration for Curry Elementary School. On this hot and sweltering day, parents filled the hallways trying to get their children registered for the new school year. George's sister, Jessica, accompanied him as he nervously awaited his turn to register for school. At seventeen, Jessica Ramos resembled her mother with big brown eyes and jet black hair. She was very mature for a young woman, and she was all business as she easily handled George's registration.

The principal appeared to be in a hurry, and assigned him to room number C-23. For some unexplained reason George felt uncomfortable with room number C-23. He kept thinking about the night his mother died and the peculiar ray of light coming from the streetlamp on 23rd street. Something did not seem right about that room number.

Surprisingly at the last moment, the principal reviewed his class assignments and reassigned him to room C-22. His teacher would be Mrs. Sylvia Sommers. Mrs. Sommers sounded like a nice name to George. Once he was registered, George ran in excitement to see Mrs. Sommers, and the classroom where he would attend school in the United States for the first time.

George had previously attended school in Mexico. The arrangement worked fine for George, since he learned Spanish at school and English at home. The school George attended in Mexico was small, neat and clean, but very different from the schools in the United States. The school in Clarkston was a two-story building with cast iron steam heaters and window swamp coolers in every room. It was also the biggest building George had ever seen in his life.

Monday morning anxiety gave way to anticipation, as the bell called the students to their assigned rooms. School was their home away from home. The students not only met new friends, but their teachers introduced them to the principles that would guide them in their future endeavors. For ten-year-old George Ramos, today was the big day. He had waited for a long time for the chance to join his older siblings at the same school.

George was a little nervous as he walked into the room. He noticed three things right away: the teacher was absent, the room was in state of disarray, and a big American flag hung in front of the room by the teacher's desk. For whatever reason, the flag made a great impression on George, and he would always remember that. He was still looking at the flag when the teacher walked in.

"Good morning, class." George turned around and gazed at the tall slender woman with a warm friendly smile. Her very presence and soft voice put George in a complete relaxed state of mind. He immediately knew that he was going to like it there.

"Good morning" they all answered.

The teacher looked over the students carefully and said, "My name is Mrs. Silvia Sommers. You may address me as Mrs. Sommers. Before we start, I want everybody to stand up."

Mrs. Sommers studied them with approval as they all stood up, almost all at the same time. They made a noise like an army drill team. Once it was quiet, she continued, "Now, with the right hand over our hearts, we will recite the Pledge of Allegiance. For those who do not know the Pledge, please follow by reading it from the blackboard."

After the class recited the Pledge, Mrs. Sommers announced that the seating arrangements would not change. George sat behind Jenny Kerns, a sweet little girl that moved to Arizona two weeks before school started. Her ocean blue eyes highlighted her pale white skin. A small patch of freckles on each side of her face, gave her the appearance of a ceramic doll. Jenny stood out like a beacon in the night.

The school days turned into weeks, and weeks turned into months. George had many things going for him. First, he could speak, read, and write Spanish and English. Second, the education he obtained while going to school in Mexico was above the level he was getting now. He felt he was ahead of the other children. The American school system of teaching was not inferior, but the system used in Mexico was much like the old European way of teaching. In Mexico, they packed as much education as they could into their students in the period between the first and six grades. They reasoned that many of the kids did not have the means to further education, so if they dropped out before high school, they would be better prepared to face the world.

George would always glance at a sign that hung above the blackboard; *THE LONGEST JOURNEY BEGINS WITH THE FIRST STEP.* George had a dream, and it was nurtured by an ardent desire to succeed. He was an intelligent, well-mannered, and friendly boy. He made many friends in his first six months of school. A popular kid with faculty members, he was well liked and always recognized by all. The more Mrs. Sommers got to know George, the more she knew there was something special about him.

CHAPTER 2

▼

Prior to becoming a teacher, Mrs. Sommers worked as a political speechwriter in Washington, DC. At thirty, she was highly regarded as one of the most knowledgeable women in American politics. She never held a political office nor did she want to run for one.

Many political hopefuls sought her services and offered her high-level positions, in Washington, but she turned them all down. She worked as a political consultant and speechwriter for five years until she became tired of the dishonesty and total disregard for constituents that most politicians manifested. She decided she needed a new life, and pursued her life long dream of became a teacher.

Sylvia first met Neil Sommers one day when she visited the Washington Municipal Library to research information about the school system in Arizona. Both were there to do research on job opportunities in the Southwest.

Over lunch, Neil told Sylvia that he graduated from the Colorado School of Mines in Denver and worked for a mining equipment manufacturing plant. He told her that he was not happy with his current job, and wanted to work in open pit mining, which was better suited for his education. His resume had made an impression. All he needed now was to interview, and the job would be his.

They met by chance at a public library, and the next thing they knew they were both heading to Arizona to pursue their dreams. They flew to Phoenix and rented a car, and drove the dusty road to Clarkston. They both fell in love with the desert as soon as they saw their first Arizona sunset fall over the giant saguaros. They loved their new jobs. Three months later, they had a small wedding in Baltimore and soon returned as permanent residents of Clarkston, Arizona.

* * * *

For almost five years, Adolf Kearns tried to impress the K's. He wanted to become a member of the K's for a long time, but he needed to show them he could be trusted. Then a chance for him to prove himself presented itself.

A big corporation was buying up land near Tuscaloosa, Alabama for a huge commercial project, and ran into trouble obtaining all the land they needed. Right in the middle of planned expansion project was a ten-acre parcel of land owned by Jimmy Otis, a proud black man. The land was not much to speak of, but it was Jimmy Otis' life. Along with his wife, Annie, and their three children, the Otis family made their meager living by selling chicken eggs and a variety of vegetables. During the holidays, they sold turkeys.

The corporation's Harvard educated lawyers could not convince the third grade educated black man to sell them the land for a nickel on the dollar. They got nowhere with him. Otis told them they were wasting their time, because he would never sell them his property, not for any amount of money.

Rumors flew through certain groups in town that the CEO of the corporation had said, unofficially, "Somebody should burn down the place and kill his animals to scare him off, or shoot the damn nigger anyway." He said it not as an order or a suggestion, but because he was madder than hell. Two weeks later, Otis and Annie were dead.

According to the local newspaper, the three Otis kids were at the local store selling a batch of the day's eggs, when someone broke into their parents' home. Mr. and Mrs. Otis both put up a struggle, but were killed as they fought off the attacker or attackers. When the kids returned home, they found their parents shot to death. The authorities announced that they would hunt down the perpetrators and bring them to justice.

Some of the people in town believed that the corporation was responsible for the crime. The black community blamed the K's for the horrendous crime. The K's themselves knew they were not guilty of the crime. However, at a town meeting held one night to discuss the crime, the speaker said, "That's one less nigger to worry about." He continued, "We will look for whoever did it, and when we find them, we will turn them over to the law. We can't let this crime hang over our heads. Plus, there is the business of the ten thousand dollar reward money."

The only man who knew exactly what happened was Adolf Kerns. Somehow, he discovered that a man offered to pay four thousand dollars to scare the Otis family into selling out. After he found the man and negotiated with him, Adolf got two thousand dollars up front. The man told him he would get the rest of the money when they sold the property.

He drove to the farm and only intended to scare the man. He did not go to kill anyone, but Otis would not scare easily. Otis ordered him off his property, and Adolf stuck an old .22 caliber pistol in his face, just to scare him. Otis grabbed the gun, and it accidentally fired, striking Otis in the chest. He fell to the floor, mortally wounded. Adolf panicked when he saw Mrs. Otis running towards him with a big kitchen knife. He fired a shot and the woman fell. With his eyes wide open in shock, Adolf froze for an instant. Otis was dead and his wife was not moving. *Think, Adolf, think.* Then he opened some drawers and threw clothing and personal belongings on the floor. He made sure he didn't leave any fingerprints, and ran out the back door.

On the way home, Adolf hoped that the authorities would think somebody was trying to rob the place. Yes, he was scared. He was damn scared. Not only were the authorities looking for whoever committed the crime, but the K's were also very much interested.

According to an acquaintance of Adolf, the black community put up ten thousand dollar reward for the capture of the guilty party. The man told Adolf, "If I were the guilty person, I would turn myself in to the authorities rather then having the K's find me first. They can make people disappear in a heartbeat."

Adolf knew just what the K's were capable of doing. He had heard many stories of people who just disappeared off the face of the earth. Even though many people knew or had an idea who was responsible for the disappearances, nobody dared report anything. They knew that some of the law enforcement officers belonged to the K's.

Adolf did not want to go to prison. He decided that his only option was to get the hell out of the area. He needed to take his family and disappear on his own, before the K's got to him. He read about a big copper mine located in southwest Arizona that was recruiting for all types of positions, and he decided Arizona was far enough for him. He packed his old pickup truck with everything he owned. Two days later, with his wife and three kids, and two thousand dollars in his pocket, Adolf Kearns was on his way to Arizona.

CHAPTER 3

▼

Sylvia Sommers was not only looking for peace and quiet in her new job, she also wanted to see if she could mold some of the young students into true and honest politicians who would work for the people they represented. She also wanted to teach them love of country, freedom, and democracy. She enjoyed her job tremendously as a small-town schoolteacher.

Classroom elections were the brainchild of Sylvia Sommers. Teachers nominated twelve students for election. Each nominee represented their classroom according to grades, attendance, neatness, personality, and popularity, in that order. In the first week of the campaign for Class President, students from each room came out with campaign posters and slogans that urged students to vote for their favorite candidate. At the end of two weeks, nine students were eliminated by a secret vote, leaving the remaining three to face the real test. The candidates now prepared for their speeches, to state their reasons why the students should elect them as President.

The finalists were Eddie Rogers, John Roberts, and George Ramos. All three scored fairly equally in all the requirements. There was a small difference, however. Eddie was a very quiet and reserved boy. Although he had many friends, his favorite pastime was reading. John Roberts, on the other hand, liked to participate in sports and group discussions. George had many friends also, but he had a problem speaking to large groups. Teachers loved him because he was very courteous and had an unequaled charisma.

One Friday after school, as George walked home, he thought about those differences. He felt good about his chances to win the school election. He was thrilled when he told his father about the upcoming school election. His family was very close-knit and everybody wanted to help George write his speech. His father told them, however, that George must write the speech himself. He explained to the children that nothing is free in life, and that they must all learn that honesty and hard work is the best policy. George knew his father was right, so he said to his brothers, "I will work on my speech all weekend, and Monday's dinner will be to celebrate my victory." With victory in mind, he went happily to his room and started to work on his speech.

Monday morning the students were excited and unable to concentrate, as they anticipated the afternoon election assembly. All morning long, George felt good about today. In the school cafeteria at lunchtime he saw Eddie, who looked very cool and unperturbed, as if nothing important was about to happen. A few minutes later, John walked in, laughing and playing with some of his friends. *How can those guys act that way knowing that in an hour we're going to be speaking in front of the whole school?* The more he thought about it the more he worried. By the time two o'clock came around, George was very jittery. *How could I brag to my brothers and sisters that I'm going to win the election, instead of thinking of what I have to say in front of all of these people!*

Finally, it was time for the speeches. George, John, and Eddie sat down on the three chairs that faced the student body. The stage was three feet high, so the trio could see the whole crowd. All eyes were on the three contestants. A thousand thoughts went through George's mind. His hands sweated, and at the same time, they were ice cold. Then he heard a voice announce his name as the first speaker. The voice he heard sounded as if it came from miles away, or from a deep hole in the ground. His knees were weak. A tremendous weight pushed down on his chest. Mrs. Sommers called his names three times before he managed to stand up. He pushed away whatever it was that held him down. At least that is what he felt.

Slowly he walked to the microphone. He grabbed it and tried to say something, but his mouth would not open. He felt as though a thousand pairs of eyes were watching him. He finally began to speak.

"Fellow students and faculty members, Today…." As he spoke, he looked down to the front row and made eye contact with a student that had a big smile on his face. *Why is that guy laughing at me?* He tried to continue his speech and looked up at the whole group, but he forgot the next word. He closed his eyes, and that made it easier to remember. He stuttered a couple of times. Then he relaxed a little and continued, and then he finally finished and sat down. His first thought was to run out of the building and never come back to school.

George fought the urge to cry as he heard Johnny's name announced. He noticed that Johnny walked to the microphone and spoke as if he was talking to a couple of his friends on the playground. Eddie was the last one to speak. As he listened to Eddie, George knew that his chances of becoming class President were diminishing with every word that Eddie spoke. After the superb speech and standing ovation for Eddie, he knew that without a doubt, Eddie had won the election before the voting even began.

Losing was very hard for George. He neglected to congratulate Eddie. After class, Mrs. Sommers asked George to stay and talk. He didn't want to face his teacher as she said to him, "George, look at me and tell me what exactly happened today. I read your speech and it was just as good as the others. It would have been up to the students to decide. What happened?"

"I don't know. It's something I can't explain. It was a weird feeling. I do know this, it will never happen again. I will never do anything again that will require me to speak in front of a group of people."

"George, whatever you have to do, follow your conscience. Face it with your head high. You did no wrong. You just didn't do everything right. Don't diminish your ability to do things because of one single incident."

George felt a little better and said, "Thank you, Mrs. Sommers. I'll see you tomorrow." As he left the room, he saw Eddie waiting there. *Probably to gloat over his victory.*

"I was waiting for you, George," Eddie said in a low tone.

"Why?" He angrily continued, "You want to rub it in?"

"No, I just want to talk to you to see if we can be friends."

"I don't feel like talking right now. Maybe tomorrow. Bye."

"Bye," said Eddie, sounding disappointed.

On the way home, George thought about what Mrs. Sommers said. He was ready to tell his family that he lost, but would try harder the next time. As he opened the front door to his house, he saw the balloons hanging all over the living room, and a big sign that read *WELCOME MR. PRESIDENT.* George stood there for what seemed like hours. Then he turned and ran to his room.

George did not want to come out of his room for supper, even though his brothers kept calling him. He was still crying when his father came into the room with a glass of milk and a sandwich. "George, here. Eat this," said his father.

"I'm not hungry."

"Come on," his father said with a gentle voice. "Eat while you tell me exactly what happened at school today." George had a lot of respect for his father, so he began to eat. He explained his earlier experience, up to the conversation he had with Eddie. After he listened to George his father said, "I believe what your teacher said has a lot of truth to it. You are giving up too easy and that is not the way I have taught you and your brothers and sisters."

His father continued, "There is no dishonor in losing. What you have to learn is that you must never underestimate your opponents. And whenever you enter any kind of competition, give it your best shot. And if you lose, do it with dignity and pride. As for your attitude towards Eddie, that was dumb. I want you to promise me that you will apologize to him and try to be his friend. Okay?"

"I promise to do what you asked. I will also promise that from now on, I will work hard, try my best and maybe someday I will run for President of the United States of America."

"That's the ticket, kid. That's the way to think," his father said as he walked out of the room.

The next morning at school, George saw Eddie sitting under a tree reading a book. He went straight to him and stood in front of Eddie. "Eddie, I want to apologize for my attitude yesterday." He looked away for a moment then said, "You were the best and you deserved to win."

"Forget it. You don't have to apologize. You didn't say any bad things to me."

"I have to. I acted dumb."

"Well, if it makes you feel better, I accept."

"Thanks, Eddie. Do you still want to be friends with me after the way I acted?"

"Of course I do."

"Then let's shake hands on it and try to be the best of friends."

"Okay," Eddie answered, as he extended his hand towards George.

After they shook hands, George smiled and told Eddie, "Let's go see Mrs. Sommers. I have something to say to her also."

Mrs. Sommers saw the two boys walk into the classroom and said, "Good morning, boys. It's a little early, isn't it?"

The boys returned the greeting, then George eagerly began to talk. "Mrs. Sommers, I thought over what you said yesterday and I decided it made a lot of sense. So I want to tell you that I accept your offer of help, on one condition."

"And what is that condition, George?"

"That you help Eddie equally, the way you help me. From now on, Eddie and I are going to be the best of friends. We will compete against each other in many things—sports, work, goals, and who knows what else." Then he turned and faced Eddie, and he said in a lower voice, "Even girls." That made him blush a little bit, and then all three of them laughed as he continued. "But no matter who wins or who loses, we are going to remain friends for the rest of our lives."

"That is great! I will help you boys in any way I can, and if your choice is to become politicians when you become adults, I promise that I will make you two the best politicians in the country."

Eddie and George became inseparable. They ate at the school cafeteria, went to movies at the local theatre, and raced each other at the public swimming pool. They were like two peas in a pod. They competed fearlessly against each other but when it was over, they remained good friends. They both loved to stand by the American flag and take turns leading the rest of the class in reciting the Pledge of Allegiance.

✳   ✳   ✳   ✳

Eddie's parents owned a trading post at the Tohono O'odham Indian Reservation, about forty miles from Clarkston. On weekends, Eddie rode with his father to take a truckload of goods to the reservation. He would ride in the back and keep an eye on all the supplies. His father did not like the idea, but the truck was a two-ton flatbed with a four-foot high rack all around it, and Eddie loved to ride there. Sometimes Eddie would invite George to go with him. Every time George went with him, he always had fun when he played with Eddie and all of his Indian friends.

One day they attended a funeral on the reservation for a friend of Eddie's father. They noticed some personal possessions were buried with the body, and some were left on top after the grave was covered. Later that day as they discussed the funeral, Eddie asked George, "If you were to die, what would be the one thing you would want most to take with you?"

"The American flag. That would be nice."

"A flag? Why would you want a flag?"

"Well, because that would mean that I had died a hero. How about you?"

"We both think the same way. I would also like a flag."

"Let's promise each other that when one of us dies, the other will make sure his friend takes an American flag with him to the grave."

"Okay by me, so let's shake hands," George said, extending his hand.

After they shook hands, Eddie said, "Remember, George, that will be our little secret." They both agreed. The school year ended and summer vacation gave George and Eddie a chance to become even closer.

CHAPTER 4

▼

When World War II began, George became fascinated with news about the war in Europe and in the Pacific theatre. He listened to the evening news on the radio whenever he could. Everyday he studied the newspaper for news on the war. He especially enjoyed viewing *Life* magazine because it carried pictures of actual combat, and on Saturday afternoons, he could hardly wait for the war footage shown during the intermission at the local theatre. George put together a scrapbook of war pictures, with stories of battles, heroes, victories, and defeats. The picture he treasured the most was the one of the Marines raising the flag at Iwo Jima.

George and Eddie battled each other in several competitions over the years, where they took turns winning the top spot. Now, before they entered high school, they faced each other for the last time, as they fought a friendly fight for the position of class President.

On Friday after school, George and Eddie walked home together. George noticed that Eddie was unusually quiet, and that he had been acting that way all day. George asked, "Are you coming to my house tomorrow so we can write our speeches together?"

"No, I have to go to the reservation with my parents. I guess I'll write mine over there."

"Are you going to beat me on Monday?"

"I don't think I will ever beat you at anything ever again."

"What makes you say that?" George asked him with a puzzled look.

"I don't know. I'm just saying that." They walked in silence for a little while, as they came to the corner where they always separated to go to their own homes.

Eddie asked, "George, do you remember the promise we made one another about the flag?"

"Sure, I remember. Why?" George had almost forgotten.

"Nothing," attempting to laugh. "I thought you might have forgotten."

George thought he actually saw tears in his eyes as Eddie turned and yelled, "See you Monday at school." That was the last time George ever saw Eddie alive.

That night, George told his father about the strange way Eddie acted. "I don't think there's anything to worry about, George. Maybe he was just thinking about the Monday election."

George went to sleep, thinking of his friend Eddie.

Monday morning George went to school earlier than usual. He began to look for his friend right away, as was his routine. He knew Eddie always came early to school, but George could not find him anywhere. George decided to check with Mrs. Sommers. George and Eddie visited her classroom every chance they had. As he entered the room, he saw Mrs. Sommers. She looked very sad. She came over to George without a word, put her arms around him, and George felt her tears hit his shoulder. George did not understand why she was acting like that and asked, "What's wrong, Mrs. Sommers?"

She wiped her eyes with a Kleenex, and answered in a voice that he could hardly hear. "You don't know what happened yesterday?"

"I have no idea what you are talking about," George answered, mystified.

"It's Eddie," she quietly answered.

"What happened to Eddie?" he shouted.

"His father had an accident coming from the reservation last night."

"Is Eddie hurt?" George asked in a weak voice.

George waited for an answer. "Eddie's father tried to miss a cow that was in the road and turned the truck over on its side." She continued, "Eddie was thrown out and his neck was broken."

In disbelief, George asked, "Is he going to be okay?" He repeated himself. He didn't understand the meaning of a broken neck.

"He died in the accident," she finally said. George felt as though a twenty-pound hammer hit him in the chest. He tried to speak but no words could come out of his mouth. He broke away from Mrs. Sommers and ran out of the room, crying all the way home.

George sat on his bed that night and cried. He fell asleep holding his little dog. The next morning, he awoke with his hands still touching the collar that Eddie bought for her. He looked at the little red heart on the collar. On one side of the heart was Shasta's name, and the American flag was on the other. George suddenly sat up and said, "The flag! Yea, the flag!" He remembered the little secret the friends shared. When they made the pact so long ago, George never imagined that it would ever come true. But no matter what, he made a promise to his best friend and he was going to keep that promise.

George was on a mission that day to get a small flag. *Where am I going to get a flag?* He went from store to store looking for a small flag and was almost ready to give up. Then he remembered that on the 4th of July last year, he and Eddie had bought two small flags. George remembered how proud they were of their flags. Very few people had them, except the ones that were in the parade. Eddie told George that day, "One of these days when we get older, you and I will see that everybody in town has an American flag on the 4th of July celebration." That was the flag George decided to use.

When it was time for the wake, George removed the small flag from its special hiding place. He folded the small flag neatly and properly in the inside pocket of his coat. He and his family walked together to the Catholic church where Eddie and George had been alter boys together. Once inside the church, he waited for his chance to do what he knew he had to do. All the kids lined up and went up to the front to view the open casket. Some touched Eddie as they paid their last respects. That gave George an idea. When all the kids passed and no one was close by, he approached the casket with the flag in his right hand. As he fought the urge to cry, he touched his friend's heart. As he did so, he slipped the flag in the coat pocket directly over Eddie's heart.

The next morning at the graveside, George kept to himself, away from the crowd. As the priest said his final words, George stared at the grave. *You said you would never beat me at anything else again. But you did! Who is going to make sure I take a flag to my grave?* The last thing he said to Eddie was, "Goodbye, friend." With that he turned around and walked back to the schoolyard. He sat there by himself all afternoon, and remembered the good times with his best friend.

As time passed, George breezed through junior high school with honors. Holding the position of class speaker was very rewarding to him, as he graduated to high school. His love for the American flag developed into love for his country. He believed very strongly in America for Americans. He also believed in a united America where there was no race or color barrier. He continued working with Mrs. Sommers, and his decision to have a future in public service made Mrs. Sommers very happy.

One day she told her husband, "This boy has the qualities to become a great public servant, and I'm going to help him prepare for the future. It is not unrea-

sonable to say that George may someday run for the highest office in the land."
That got a smile from her husband.

*　　　*　　　*　　　*

Hanson Kerns was born in Alabama. His father was a German-American, a
self-proclaimed racist, a known wife beater, and a drunk. His only friends were
scum and the dregs of society. Hans was the oldest of the three Kerns children.
From the time he was old enough to walk, he always carried a toy wooden rifle.
The family's move to the Arizona desert did not deter Hans' love for guns. The
wide-open spaces gave him more freedom to play with toy guns. One day, as he
played in an old abandoned house, he found a five-dollar gold coin. He used the
coin to buy his very own BB gun.

Adolf Kerns, Hans' father, worked at the big open pit copper mine. His lifestyle did not change with the new steady job, but now he had more money to get
drunk more often. He had even less friends than when he lived in Alabama. The
beatings to his wife, Julie, became more frequent and more severe, until she
decided she had enough. The very next time he came home drunk and began to
beat her, she had Jenny, her daughter, call the law.

When the officers arrived, Adolf tried to grab a pistol he kept hidden in the
closet. The officers, Sergeant Neto Garcia, a Mexican-American, and Bryan
Lewis, a Tohono O'odham Indian, guessed his intentions and wrestled him to
the floor. Hanson watched as his father fought with the police. He went outside
and returned with his BB gun, and began shooting at the officers. His mother
quickly took the gun away from him. Sergeant Garcia handcuffed Adolf and took
him to jail.

Three days later, Julie paid Adolf's bail so he would not lose his job. After
Jenny drove him home, he stormed into the living room and screamed, "Bitch,
you did it this time. I got dragged to jail by a damn greaser and a blanket ass
Indian. White people don't tolerate that kind of treatment. Dirty bitch, you
made your bed. Now sleep on it. I'm getting the fuck out of here." He packed
some of his things, slammed the front door on his way out, and was never heard
from again.

Hanson missed his father. He never forgot the day he shot at the police officers with his BB gun. He had tried to help his father and now wished he had a real
rifle that night. He was older now and owned a real rifle. He had become an
obsessive gun fanatic, and whenever he got the chance, he took his younger
brother Bruno out to the desert for target practice. They shot countless rounds of

ammunition. By the time he entered high school, he was a crack shot. Deadly accurate at 200 yards with his Winchester 270, Hanson could center a "bull's eye" with remarkable consistency. Guns made him feel superior and many times he felt the urge to shoot somebody someday. Sometimes, in his dark bedroom, he pointed his fully loaded rifle at unsuspecting passersby. He followed them with the crosshairs of his scope until they were out of sight.

Because he was bigger than most kids in his class, he could whip any of them in a heartbeat. He hated Mexicans and Indians, but the one he hated the most was his sister's boyfriend. He hated George Ramos with a passion and had beaten him up several times in the past. Every time he hit George, he would say to him, "I don't want to catch you with my sister again. Every time I catch you with her I'll stomp the shit out of you again."

Jenny told her mother about the fights many times, but her mother could not do anything about it. She could not control her son, Hanson. Actually, she was becoming increasingly afraid of him. Hanson blamed his mother for his father running out on them and he told her that every day.

George was not a troublemaker and certainly not a fist fighter, but he had no fear of anything or anybody, no matter how big they were. After their last fight, George told Jenny that he would not tolerate the beatings anymore. He told her, "Next time he comes at me, I will do everything in my power to defend myself and fight back." George had grown taller and stronger in the last year. He took boxing lessons from his uncle Roger, a professional boxer who had retired with an outstanding boxing career record. George's older brothers were also tired of seeing him come home beaten up, so they decided to teach him how to defend himself.

It was not long before Hanson caught George and Jenny together at the local park. It was the 4th of July and a large crowd of people had gathered there for the celebration. Jenny saw Hanson coming towards them and stood between George and her brother. "Hanson, why can't you leave us alone? George doesn't want to fight. We are not doing anything wrong." Hanson pushed her roughly aside, and threw her on the grass.

Hanson stared at George and said, "I told you, you damn greaser. My sister is not going to go around with no bean eater as long as I'm around. You don't learn, do you? This time you better learn because I'm going to break both your legs." George looked at Jenny on the ground with tears in her eyes and did not need a formal invitation. He jumped into combat with the rage of a wounded bear.

The fight lasted about a minute and a half and hundreds of people watched. The firefighters finally broke it up. When it was over, it was Hanson who was on the ground with a bloody nose and mouth. He lost a front tooth and both his eyes were black and blue. Hanson got up very slowly and said to George, "This is not the end, Greaser. The next time we meet, you are a dead fucking Mexican."

That night Hanson secretly packed some of his things and ran away from home. He did not have much to pack, but he made sure that his knife, his four-inch barrel 22 H&R revolver, and ammunition were in his travel bag.

He caught a ride out of town in a truck traveling to Wickenburg, Arizona, where he hopped on a train going west to California. Hanson had the railroad boxcar to himself for a while. Somewhere along the way, the train slowed down as it approached a water station, and a hobo jumped in. The train regained speed and the hobo moved closer to the corner where Hans sat in the shadows. At first, the hobo feigned friendliness. After a while though, he figured that the Hanson was but a young boy. He shouted and tried to act tough.

"Move out of that corner," he told the teenager. "I want that spot." Hans reluctantly grabbed his bag and started to move. "And leave that bag there!" yelled the hobo.

"Stay away from me and my stuff and quit bothering me," Hans answered nervously. The bum didn't stop, and crept towards Hanson. "Stay away! Stay away!" Hans shouted.

The hobo continued to ease towards Hanson. Hans was terrified and figured he had to do something fast. He jerked the H&R from his bag, raised it, and fired twice, all in one motion. The hobo stood motionless, with his eyes wide open. He fell to his knees and shrieked, "You dirty bastard!" Then he hit the wooden floor and begun to moan, moving from side to side. Blood flowed from the hole in his stomach.

Hans was in shock and his body quivered with fear. Slowly he began to realize what had transpired in just a few seconds. When he regained his ability to reason and understand, he moved away from the man on the floor. Hans went to the farthest corner of the swaying boxcar, sat down, and began to bang his head over and over against the boxcar wall. After a few minutes he stopped, and began to think of what to do next. The *tap tap tap* noise of the steel wheels as they hit the joints of the rails was hypnotizing to Hans. Hans was now in a trance as he fought to figure things out. *One thing for sure, no one can find me in this boxcar with a dead man.* He decided to jump out of the boxcar as soon as the train slowed down.

The opportunity came ten minutes later. As the train came into a station in a small town, it slowed down enough for Hans to jump. He slid the heavy door open and found that it was beginning to get dark. When he lived in Alabama, he had seen tramps jump off slow-moving trains many times. He closed his eyes and jumped, and was successful to some degree, thanks to some grass and a big bush that grew close to the tracks. All the damage he could find were some small patches of skin missing from his knees and elbows, and a sore arm. He smiled and congratulated himself. *Way to go, Hans.* He turned to see what looked like a train depot as he walked to town.

Hans disappeared for two weeks, and resurfaced in Los Angeles with twenty-five dollars in his pocket. The money came from the sale of his old H&R gun and a pocketknife he sold to a taxi driver. The same man got Hans a temporary job mowing lawns in Riverside, California. How he got to the city of Los Angeles was not important, he thought. What was important to him was what to do now.

Hans was hungry and looked for a place where he could buy something to eat. He saw a hot dog stand half way down the block and headed for it. After he ate a hot dog and drank a coke, he felt better, and again began to think of what to do next. Twenty minutes later, the answer came to him.

Across the street was an Army Recruiting Station and that gave him an idea. He did not go in right away. He waited for two hours, thinking about the man he left bleeding in the boxcar. *Is the law looking for me? If somebody saw me walking away from the tracks, could they finger me?* Then he concluded that without money and not knowing the city, his best bet was to disappear by enlisting in the U.S. Army. He walked in. *I look old enough.* The sergeant looked at him and asked smiling, "Are you ready to become a man?"

"I am a man," was the answer.

"Good, good, that is what we need here." The sergeant moved some papers, looked in Hans' eyes and asked, "Where are you from?"

"From here, there, and nowhere," Hans said, trying not to sound like a wise-ass, but trying to conceal the fact that he was making things up. He continued, "From an orphanage to foster homes and now out the world looking for a job. I think this is as good a job as any." The sergeant did not believe a word he said, but he didn't give a shit either. All he wanted was to get his daily quota and to hell with the rest. Hanson Kerns changed his name to Hans Kros and become a soldier in the United States Army.

CHAPTER 5

▼

In 1950, North Korea invaded the Republic of South Korea. The United States, along with the rest of United Nations, started sending troops to defend South Korea in what some called a "Police Action."

One of George's brothers volunteered in the United States Army, and had been in Korea for about seven months. In his high school Political Science and History classes, discussions of the Korean War were sometimes heated and argumentative, and George always managed to be in the middle of the arguments. He reasoned that the United States should help any country that was threatened by a Communist country, not only for that country's sake, but for our protection as well. He knew that the Communist threat was very evident all over the world. But his best argument was that in time of war, we should all be tightly united behind our own country's policies. Some of the other students believed that that we had no business over there, and should stay out of it.

One day during one of these discussions, a student asked George, "If you believe so much in what you are saying, why don't you join the Army and go help fight that war?"

"I think I will," was the answer, and everybody laughed. Later that evening, he told Mrs. Sommers that he made the decision to join the Army.

"No, George, you are not going to do such a thing. You are just a boy. You have many things going for you. I do not think your father is going to give you permission to go anyway. You know at your age he has to sign for approval."

"He'll sign," George answered.

"What about graduating from high school? Your career?"

"High school can wait until I get back. As for my career, if I am going to be a public servant, I should start by serving my country first."

"What does Jenny say about your idea of joining the Army?"

"I haven't told her yet. I'm going to tell her tonight."

"Well, all I can say is that I'm opposed to it, but you have to do whatever you think is best for you."

Nobody could say that George's decision to enlist in the U.S. Army was an act of bravado. He wasn't a show-off and his intentions were legitimate. The whole class was aware of the Korean War, and George felt it was his duty to enlist. There were two things that might prevent him from enlisting in the army; he needed a little over a year to finish high school, and he wasn't eighteen years old yet. He figured that high school could wait until he came back, or he could finish it in the army. As for his age, he looked old enough and had the size, five foot nine inches tall, 168 lbs with a very muscular body. The tough part was convincing his father.

As George waited for Jenny to walk her home, he was thinking of the best way to approach his father. He needed Jenny to help him convince his father. He was confident that in the end everything would work out. George he had a big smile on his face and a twinkle in his brown eyes as he thought about how his black curly hair would look like after the Army barbers were done with him.

For an hour and a half, George and Jenny discussed his decision to enlist in the Army. Finally, George said, "Jenny, you have to understand. To me, joining the Army is something that I feel I have to do."

"Is there anything I can say that will make you change your mind?"

"Jenny, you know that I love you very much. But ever since the war started in Korea, the idea of enlisting has been eating at me right here," he said, doubling his right fist and tapping his heart. "It's weird."

"How does your father feel about it?"

"I have been working on him for a week, but he won't budge."

"So what are you going to do? You can't enlist without his permission?"

"I'll cross that bridge when I come to it. Tomorrow I will ask him one more time and I want you to be there when I do."

"I'll be there, but I won't agree with everything you're saying. I would be lying to him."

＊   ＊   ＊   ＊

"George, I know you mean well, but you are too young to enlist. Why don't you wait until after you graduate?" George's father said. The doorbell rang and George opened the door.

George acted surprised and said, "Hi, Jenny, come on in."

Jenny smiled, and looked at George's father as she asked, "Am I interrupting anything?" She almost blushed. She knew what was going on.

"I'm trying to see if I can get George to forget this silly notion he has of enlisting in the Army before he finishes high school. It doesn't make any sense."

"Dad, I know it doesn't make sense to you, but there is something telling me that enlisting is what I have to do. I was really hoping you would understand."

"I must be crazy, but because I know you are a level headed guy, I'll sign. You have the right to determine your own future, but please try to reconsider your decision."

"I wish that I could, but my mind is made up. Thanks, Dad." Turning to face Jenny he continued, "I promise both of you that as soon as I get back, I will finish high school." He saw Jenny's eyes fill with tears and added, "Don't worry. I may not have to go to Korea. I could be sent anywhere else in the world."

＊   ＊   ＊   ＊

For the conscripts, the novelty of being in uniform soon wore out. They made it through basic training, shaping up because they were young and full of vigor. As the war escalated and the Army needed more troops in Korea, combat training became harder and rougher and the cadre became pushier. For George, who was a volunteer, every obstacle and every lesson was a welcomed challenge and he tried his best. That was his way.

One day as George walked back to base, he noticed two civilians dragging the American flag on the ground. He caught their attention when he said, "That is no way to treat the flag, guys."

They turned to look at him and answered, "Who the hell are you? What the hell do you care what we do with this piece of shitty rag?"

"Who I am doesn't matter, but I'll be courteous and tell you anyway. My name is Ramos and I have been taught to never treat the flag in that manner."

"This is nothing but a piece of cloth," said the punk as he held the flag up above his head. "And you are nothing but a nosy Mexican trying to play hero."

"I am an American and you should know that every American needs to learn to respect the symbol of our freedom and democracy."

"Well here is what I think of this piece of shit," he snapped back, and threw the flag on the ground and stomped on it.

George grabbed the man's arm and threw him to the ground. The other man joined the fight and they beat George to a bloody pulp. The MP's found him on the ground, covered with blood with the flag on top of him.

After boot camp and another month of specialized training, George received his orders to ship out. The word was that most of the outfit was headed for Germany, but they needed some volunteers for combat duty in Korea. George was one the first one to volunteer. As George entered the office of Lieutenant O'Donnell, who was interviewing the volunteers, he looked at George and said, "You're a little young, aren't you?"

"Yes, Sir," was the reply.

"Why do you wish to volunteer?"

George answered loud and clear, "Because I am a soldier in the United States Army, Sir." The Lieutenant looked at him for a little while and thought, "God knows they're all young." Then he said, "That will be all, Soldier." George saluted, turned around, and went out the door smiling.

*   *   *   *

George had two weeks of leave before he was scheduled to ship out. He used the time to visit his family, friends, his high school sweetheart, and Mrs. Sommers. His former teacher was very happy to see him. As she stood at the door and said her last goodbye, George noticed tears in her eyes. He told her, "Mrs. Sommers, I want you to know that I appreciate very much all you have done for me. When I get back, and I am coming back, we will continue working together, if you like."

"I know. I have the feeling we will be working together for a long time."

On his last night of leave, Jenny and her family invited George to their home for dinner. Afterwards, they sat alone together, and discussed their plans for the future. George felt as if time was moving at the speed of sound. Before he left her house, they kissed. Then George told her, "Jenny, I love you very much. I really hope you wait for me."

"I will wait for you for as long as it takes," she replied.

At George's home, it had been two weeks of happiness and laughter, but at the bus depot that morning, it was tears and sadness. On the bus ride back to the base, he remembered his father's last words, "Try to locate your brother if you have the chance. Both of you take very good care of yourselves and get back safe and sound. I love you guys very much. God bless you both."

*   *   *   *

When the Marines landed and captured the port of Inchon, the soldiers from the 10th Corps entered the port directly behind the Marines. This cleared the way for General Walker's troops to fight their way out of the Pusan Perimeter, inflicting heavy losses on the enemy. Then they joined the 10th Corps near Seoul.

Ships arrived and unloaded their cargos of men and supplies in Pusan. As fast as they hit the Korean soil, troops from the 1st Battalion of the 19th Infantry, along with other units, began their march north. Many were green and untried troops, but they soon would learn the hard lessons of battle or die trying. Young men became hardened veterans fast.

The push north from the Pusan Perimeter to the 38th Parallel and beyond became a rout. The North Koreans were pushed back without great difficulty. For young George Ramos of the 19th Infantry, things were moving fast. He was promoted to corporal in his first month in Korea. He was involved in many skirmishes and was slightly wounded in his left leg.

The enemy was on the run. To most of the men in the lines, this war would soon be over. Rumors were that they would all be home for Christmas. In October and November, more than 300,000 Chinese troops crossed into North Korea. Hopes for a quick end to the war soon disappeared. The Chinese struck so fast and so suddenly that our intelligence did not have a clue as to their numbers or area of attack. Consequently, American, South Korean, and U.N. troops were caught off guard, especially those that were deep inside the 38th Parallel, and were forced to retreat.

Truce talks began in July, but the fighting was not over by any means. Neither side made any important gains, but they fought many hard and bitter battles for strategic positions. Some of these battles included Pork Chop Hill, Bloody Ridge, Old Baldy and other hills; thus, the war was sometimes called the "Battle for the Hills." It was here that George earned the Silver Star, two more Purple Hearts and another battlefield promotion.

Korea taught George many things, but if his future was going to be in politics, Korea turned out to be a crucible of unlimited opportunities to learn of our government's foreign policies.

CHAPTER 6

▼

The rifle-shooting contest was the brainchild of General Benton Hightower. General Hightower was a highly decorated soldier who lost an eye in battle, just before the surrender of Germany. He loved rifle-shooting matches, and over the years, he participated in many events, and had even won a few. He was an expert shot, but the loss of his right eye abruptly ended his shooting competition days. As Commander of the Seventh Army in Europe, General Hightower believed that rifle marksmanship was essential to the Army, even in peacetime. So he formed a company of the best rifle sharpshooters to be used as snipers.

For a while, shooting competition was limited to the members of the company. Later, the General challenged any outfit in the United States Armed Forces. When nobody could beat his boys, he decided that competition against soldiers from other countries would be fun. He introduced the idea to commanders from the other countries. The notion took off like wildfire, and soon soldiers from France, West Germany, Italy, and other military units from the United States eagerly signed up. The Army promoted the event as a way to train their own teams for the Olympics. Thus the "Eagle Eye Shooters Contest" was born.

This was the fourth year of the contest. The Americans lost the first two years, but last year, thanks to a newcomer in the group, the Americans took the trophy. This year, General Hightower was so sure of victory, that he literally bet his rent money on an American win. Sergeant Jack Johnson, who was responsible for the sniper company's performance, assured the General that the six soldiers assigned to the contest were the best in all of Europe.

The day before the shooting match, Sergeant Johnson instructed the team on the importance of going to bed early, getting up early, and eating a good breakfast. "Absolutely no drinking the night before," he ordered. He told the team that he had personally guaranteed the General a victory, and by God, he was going to get it. Everybody agreed and were very enthusiastic about the upcoming event, all except Hans. Hans knew he was the best marksman the team ever had. His unerring marksmanship had carried the team to victory many times before, and he was certain he could do it again tomorrow. In Hans' mind, it was just another walk in the park.

Hans was a loner and the other men on the team knew it, so they kept out of his way. At first, they tried to befriend him, but he wouldn't have any of it. Every night before bedtime, Hans walked outside the barracks and sat alone for a few hours. By the time he came back in, everybody was asleep.

That night, he again sat outside alone. *I can't stand that stupid nigger giving me orders, especially telling me what I should or shouldn't do on my own time. I'm going to go out and drink and to hell with Johnson.* Instead of returning to his bunk, he set out walking to town.

The Le Vent Blanc Bar was Hans' favorite place, because the people that drank there kept to themselves. He did not drink hard the way his father did. He nursed a few beers for hours, thinking of his family back home. *Home, I haven't got a home.* But as the night wore on, his thoughts came back to Johnson. The more he thought about Johnson, the drunker he got. He had never been drunk before in his whole life, but his dislike for Johnson fueled his anger, until in a drunken stupor, he decided not to go back to the base. *I'll never go back. I'll stay AWOL. Screw that nigger and his shooting matches.*

Hans did not return to base that night and his replacement had not been good enough for their group to win. The best they could do was third place in a competition of ten groups. As the Italian team accepted the first place trophy, Johnson saw General Hightower give him a dirty look. He knew he was in trouble as he mumbled, "I'm in deep shit now."

That night Johnson went looking for Hans. He paced from bar to bar, searching for the traitor who had cost his team the victory. Finally, he spotted him in the Le Vent Blanc Bar. "There that bastard is," the Sergeant muttered, madder than hell. He walked over to the table where Hans sat drinking. He yelled, "Kiss me, you son of a bitch! Come on kiss me!" He pointed at his own face as he screamed.

Hans was shaky and nervous, and did not know what to do. He asked him, "What are you, nuts?

"No," answered Johnson, and grabbed Hans by the throat. "I just like to get kissed when I get screwed, you bastard!" Johnson threw Hans to the floor and yelled all kinds of obscenities, as he punched and kicked him furiously. Hans tried to defend himself, but Johnson was too much for him. The Sergeant gave him the worst beating of his life. As Johnson left the bar, Hans laid there bleeding from the mouth, nose, ears, and both sides of his face. All he thought of now were the words the Sergeant whispered in his ear before he left. "You screwed up royally, asshole. It's the stockade for you."

No one intervened. No one said anything. You could hear a pin drop in the silence that ensued. Then from a dark corner of the room, a man stood up and walked towards Hans. He witnessed the whole episode, and not by accident. He had been watching Hans all evening. Only when Johnson left, did he approach Hans. He picked up his hat, helped him up, and took him to the dark corner table. The two men talked quietly for a few minutes, and soon walked out of the place together. Walking was an excruciating effort for Hans, but with help from the stranger, he accomplished the task.

That night forever changed Hans' life. He knew the penalty for being AWOL, and decided he did not want any time in the brig. Besides, his new acquaintance had offered him a way out of France. Hans told his friend that he would go with him, but first he wanted to get even with that black bastard who whipped him.

Two weeks later, a prostitute found Sergeant Johnson dead in the parking lot of a red light district bar. Johnson had been shot once in the head. His wallet, ring, and watch were missing. The French authorities decided it was just another robbery/murder incident that was quite common in that area. They warned the military that Johnson knew this part of the city was off-limits to the U.S. military personnel and should not have been there. With that, they closed the case.

*   *   *   *

Karlos (the Jackal, as he was known to Interpol) knew that Interpol was dangerously close on his trail. He also knew that in his business, very few ever made it to retirement. Some were serving life sentences in different countries, but the majority were dead and buried. Being an assassin for hire paid handsomely but it was not a romantic, safe, or exciting occupation. However, there was one thing that was interesting to Karlos—the fact that people like him were needed all over the world. He laughed. *You'd sure be surprised to know the kind of people that hire assassins.*

Karlos thought of somehow duplicating himself. *Yes, that would do it, but it won't be easy.* He needed something to throw the Interpol off his trail before he retired. *I just have a year or two left. I'd better get started.*

One day while watching a military rifle-shooting contest, he saw this young American soldier. Karlos was highly impressed with the shooting ability of the young man. Since the shooting matches were open to the public, Karlos watched him every chance he got.

The American soldier resembled Karlos and was even similar in build. He found out that the soldier's favorite place to drink was the Le Vent Blanc Bar, and watched him from a dark corner. It did not take long for Karlos to figure out that the soldier was a loner. *Perfect. Now I have to find a way to approach him.* His opportunity came two nights later.

After the fight, Karlos took Hans to his place. He cleaned him up, doctored his wounds, and fed him. After a few days at Karlos' place, Hans got restless. So Karlos asked him, "Are you planning to go back to the base?"

"No," Hans answered. "The only thing I want is to kill that damned nigger."

Karlos wanted to be sure and asked, "Are you sure you want to do that? Because if you really mean it, I can help you."

Hans did not hesitate. "Damn right I want to."

Karlos thought for a moment, then said, "Okay, but I'll tell you. Once we do that, we must leave France. I have a place in Africa where nobody knows we exist. I'll have to get you papers, passport, and a new ID."

Karlos also had a job for him, but that could wait until he was sure Hans had it in him to kill a man. After two weeks, they were on their way to northern Africa.

*   *   *   *

Hans slowly moved the rifle until the crosshairs in the scope found the tiny round target mark on the silhouette. He held his breath for an instant, and gently squeezed the trigger. The noise that came from the silencer was quieter than the noise made by an air pellet gun. "Bull's eye!"

Hans heard a voice behind him. "I believe you are finally ready." Hans picked up the spotting scope and walked off.

Hans had been training for a year and a half, always under the watchful eye of Karlos, and with the best rifles, scopes, and silencers in the world. His friend had them specially made by an outlaw German gunsmith. Even though the distances were always 50, 70, or 100 meters, Hans never missed the target.

The shooting was the last phase of his training, which also included learning to speak French and German, disguising his appearance, and evasion. He also learned some personal first aid for bullet wounds, and many other little things a lone man on the run might need in order to survive. It was not an option to be mediocre at any of his training lessons. He had to be as good as or better than his instructor. As Hans disassembled the rifle, he made sure that the scope, the silencer, and other parts of the gun were clean. As he carefully put the rifle away, the man repeated, "Yes, I believe you are ready." The mentor had returned.

Karlos had a 150-acre plantation-like property, one hundred miles west of Talbelbala, Algeria, and southeast of the Atlas Mountains by the Qued Draa River that borders Morocco with Algeria. It was there that Hans found out who his benefactor was, what he did for a living, and what the job offer was. Since he had already killed one man, or maybe even two, since he wasn't sure if the man he shot the night he ran away from home had died, he decided. *Hey, why not do it for money?* Besides, he had already promised one man that the next time he saw him, he would kill him. Hans figured he had no choice anyway. If he turned the offer down, he would be signing his own death warrant. He knew too much. His life as an assassin had begun.

CHAPTER 7

▼

The dismissal of General McArthur made one of the biggest impacts on the American public. The limited war policies of the United States and the United Nations left 150,000 Americans dead or wounded. The United States, the most powerful nation in the world, had been muzzled, checked by its own strength. George could never figure out a reason for that. He could also not figure out why our country appeared to have forgotten the men in uniform that were freezing, sweltering, or dying in Korea, while they were doing their job to try to halt the spread of communism. The Korean War later became known as the "Forgotten War."

In July of 1953, the fighting stopped, but the war had not ended. The armistice was a bitter pill to swallow for some of the commanders. They declared that without total victory, an armistice should not have been signed.

George served with pride and dedication, and came out of the Korean War a very mature young man. He left the service with the rank of Lieutenant, a commission earned on the battlefield, not bad for a young man that dropped out of high school at age 16 to join the United States Army.

It bothered him, however, the way the American public reacted to the war and to the American servicemen who fought in Korea. He thought that the unity of our country that was very evident during World War II, was nonexistent in the Korean War. In his opinion, the United States government made many mistakes with their war policies.

Civilian life was the most important topic of discussion among the GI's leaving Korea, but adjusting to it was not so easy for the majority of them. For George, his return to his small hometown where everybody knew everybody else

was a piece of cake. He decided to go to work at the copper mine, the only industry in town, where generations of families worked until they retired or died.

The townspeople considered George a hero. Wherever he went, people
wanted to shake his hand. He did not want people to call him a hero. One day, as
a reporter from the local newspaper interviewed him, he was asked, "Do you con-
sider yourself a hero?"

The question irritated George. He answered, "The only heroes that I know of
are the ones that were killed on the battlefield and never made it home." He did
not talk to people about Korea, not even to his family. To some of the soldiers
that served with him in Korea, however, he was a hero. Three soldiers returned
from Korea only because George's courage and guts saved them from certain
death. Unbeknownst to him, they petitioned the United States Army to award
George the Medal of Honor. So far, the Army had denied their request, citing
lack of documentation. The only soldier that had documents to support the rec-
ommendation was Captain Roberto Medina, who was killed in action in the
"Battle for the Hills."

George was again seeing Jenny, his high school sweetheart. One night as they
sat outside and discussed their future, Jenny noticed that George was unusually
quiet. "George, what is the matter with you? Is something wrong?"

"No, it's just that I don't feel that working at the mine my entire life is what I
want. I don't know if you understand this, but deep down I feel that there's
something else out there for me."

"What do you intend to do?" she asked.

"Well, I need an education, but I can't quit my job because I will need money
to go to school. What I saved while I was in the service and my mustering-out
pay is not enough to pay for a full college education. There has to be a way."

George finished high school while he was in the Army. That made it easy for
him to enroll in the University of Arizona extension courses in Clarkston. That
decision made Mrs. Sommers very happy. It proved to her, once more, that
George had it in him to become a good public servant.

With the end of the Korean War, the American public was bracing for a reces-
sion that loomed on the horizon. Jobs were getting scarce, factories were closing
down, and the unemployment lines were getting longer. At the mine, where lay-
offs were unheard of, the working hours for the miners were shortened in order
to keep all employees working. That kept the town going.

George kept up with his studies for a while with correspondence and extension courses. Later at Mrs. Sommers' suggestion, he began studying on campus at
the University of Arizona.

George and two other miners were on a special program set up by the mining company for those that wanted to improve their education. They took turns driving to Tucson, 134 miles away. Their work schedule at the mine, combined with going to Tucson three times a week, was tiresome for the three young men. But George did not complain. He even found time to teach karate at the high school two nights a week.

By this time, George was very well known in Clarkston. Since election time was just around the corner, it did not surprise him when Mrs. Sommers called him one night. "George, the time has come for you to get serious about your political career. There is a position for Precinct Committee Member coming up. You start at the bottom with no pay, but with your studies in Political Science and Government Law, plus your popularity in town, you'll be a cinch for the job. The position will not interfere with your studies or the job at the mine."

George was easily elected. The position presented no real challenge for George. He served well and with enthusiasm. Later on, when the local Justice of the Peace suddenly passed away of a heart attack, the Town Council appointed George to serve the remainder of the term until the next election. George then decided to work his plan for the 4th of July celebration, which was three weeks away.

George enlisted his karate students to help the VFW build a float for the parade. The theme, *Lest We Forget*, was represented by the lifting of the flag at Iwo Jima. George drove to Phoenix and found a warehouse with a surplus of over 7,000 small handheld American flags, perfect for a parade. He made an offer and purchased all of the flags for a good price. He wanted to unite the community and have a good 4th of July celebration. He discussed the idea with the local organizations, who all responded favorably. George had no idea that his coming celebration would be the best his town had ever seen.

George talked to veterans and advertised in the local paper. He invited anyone who had ever been in any branch of the military to wear his or her uniform, and march in the parade. The response was greater that he could have ever imagined.

The Boy Scouts passed out flags all over town. All along the parade route, "Old Glory" flew proudly. Every man, woman, and child waved an American flag from every house, building, and street corner.

George invited a friend of his from Tucson to come to Clarkston to cover the festivities. George knew Bryan Wilson from Korea. He was a photographer for *Life* magazine and after the war moved to Tucson to work for the *Arizona Daily Star*.

George playfully told him the 4th of July celebration was going to be the best in any town in the whole USA. Bryan agreed to come because of his friendship with George. Little did he know that George was one hundred percent right.

Three Medal of Honor recipients were in the parade, one from World War I, one from World War II, and one from the Korean War. They carried the American flag that lead the parade. The first float was the Veterans of Foreign Wars' lifting of the flag at Iwo Jima, followed by the high school band. The float was beautiful, very well constructed, very original, and had a lot of detail. Parade watchers declared that the float would have won first prize in any parade in the country.

Following the floats were the men and women in uniform, all sizes, shapes and colors, young and old. There was one thing they and the people alongside of the parade route had in common. *It was good to be an American.* The pride and patriotism could clearly be seen. There was no doubt, however, that the main attraction was the sea of American flags.

While he recorded the event with his camera, Bryan felt the excitement, as he observed what national pride and unity of purpose could do for a town, its people, and a nation. The parade ended in the center of town in front of the park, and by that time, the park was filled with people. All around the park were booths, and patrons stood in line to buy burritos, hot dogs, and soft drinks. Some booths had games, and some had trinkets and other mementos for sale, but they were all decorated with red, white, and blue crepe.

In the middle of the park, there was a sixty-foot flagpole. As the color guard began to raise the flag, the entire crowd came to a complete silence. When the flag finished its climb to the top of the flagpole, the roar and clapping of hands could be heard for miles. Then the band began playing *America the Beautiful* and every man, woman, and child started to sing. As they sang, George noticed that everybody, including himself, had tears running down their faces, as they held and caressed their small flags manifesting the reverence the flag conveyed.

Bryan became a celebrity as his pictures made national news. Television stations, newspapers, and magazines around the nation carried the pictures and story. The town of Clarkston was now on the map.

George felt good because he remembered the words his childhood best friend said when they were kids. "When we get older, you and I will see that everybody carries an American flag on the 4th of July."

It took George three and half years to finish school and get his degree. With Jenny's and Mrs. Sommers' help and occasional push, he graduated with honors in the top five percent of his class.

*   *   *   *

George married Jenny one year before he finished school. The wedding was a simple home ceremony. George's and Jenny's families, Mr. And Mrs. Sommers, and two of his best friends all attended. At the dinner, when all the toasts and congratulations were done, Mrs. Sommers asked George about his plans for the future. "Mrs. Sommers, I make a good living writing speeches for politicians, but I'm thinking of running for State Senator."

"That's my boy," Mrs. Sommers said laughing.

His father stood up, lifted his glass, and said, "To the next State of Arizona Senator, George S. Ramos!"

Everybody stood up, glass in hand, "To the next Senator!" That was the serious start of George's political career.

CHAPTER 8

▼

George was smart enough to know that the biggest problem he faced in the run for State Senator had to be money. Contrary to the usual practice, and against the counsel of his advisers, he decided not to accept any money from special interest groups, but would not mind if they wanted to help in any other way. George felt that if he won, he wanted to start with a clean slate.

In a town meeting, he announced his candidacy and his platform. He also asked the community and all of the town organizations for their help and support. The response was more than he hoped for. The town was solidly behind his efforts to become State Senator. He promised to visit every single town and city in Arizona, to work hard, and to eventually win.

A wealthy Republican Senator had recently announced his retirement. Another Republican, also with very deep pockets, was preparing to run for the vacant seat. George was a Democrat, but the Democratic Party believed that George was too young and inexperienced. With the two very good politicians the Democratic Caucus had already singled out, the Democratic Party had a chance to break the stronghold the Republicans had on the Senate. The only thing left for George to do, was to run as an Independent. Both Republicans and Democrats soon began to say, "George who? An Independent running for what?"

The run for State Senator was very strenuous and at the same time very exciting. George enjoyed every minute of it. For the first time in his life, he was in a real political battle. After all, he had been well groomed for the job for most of his young life. Now it was up to George to show the public that he was the right man for the job.

George went out to cities and towns with vigor and a strong resolution. He knocked on doors. He spoke in schools, union halls, parks, and meetings of different organizations. He even gave a speech at a Boy Scout camp. He would talk to anybody that was ready to listen. People began to notice. They loved the way he was able to deliver the speeches he wrote himself. They admired the smooth and gracious way he talked. The voice, body language, and resolve of this handsome young blue color worker mesmerized the crowds. Most of all, they liked the way this charismatic young man told the truth.

In the end, he won. No, he trashed his opponents.

The celebration for his first real political victory was short and sweet. George and Jenny moved to Phoenix, the capital of Arizona. Neither one liked the idea of living in the city. They missed their small town life but they knew it went with the job.

George started the job as a green and wet-behind-the-ears young man with many expectations. Soon he found out why some of the best-known politicians were up to their knees in mud. He stayed clean, did a good job, and was re-elected to a second term.

George was the first Independent candidate ever elected Senator in the state of Arizona. Now both the Republican and Democratic parties noticed the way people were attracted to him. They began to court him. Both parties knew that a man like George could do wonders for their party. George kept doing his job as well as he could. He was not interested in politics per se; he was interested in the people he served.

George's experience as a Senator for the state of Arizona was good for George's future political career. George gained national recognition when he introduced legislation that penalized unfair labor practices to minorities in the mines in Arizona such as the dual wage system that his father had endured. He became an outspoken advocate for abolishment of all forms of segregation against Mexican Americans that were still in practice in certain southwest communities. Labor unions unanimously endorsed his views. George did not forget his upbringing. He became the working man's political ally.

In the meantime, the sound of war drums was once again in the air, this time in Vietnam. It was not long before the United States was heavily involved in yet another unpopular war.

As an Army Reserve officer with combat experience, George soon found himself with a Ranger unit deep in the jungles of Vietnam. The Rangers' job was to raise havoc behind enemy lines, a very dangerous job. The Rangers were dropped off in small groups, deep behind enemy lines for search-and-destroy operations.

For George Ramos, this war was different in many ways from the Korean War. There were never heavy concentrations of forces on either side shooting at each other. The terrain in Vietnam was mostly hot, rotten-smelling jungles, compared to Korea's mountains and open country. Except for the huge American bombing raids, the fighting was mostly guerrilla warfare.

In the United States, the nation was divided. Many Americans believed that the United States' involvement in the war was necessary. But many others felt it was unnecessary and wrong. Even though the young draftees were very brave and fought hard, there were many malcontents. The news from the States about the "draft card burners" gave the malcontents reason to feel that the United States had no business in Vietnam and caused the military many problems. Serious problems arose, like the "fragging" of officers, mostly due to the heavy use of drugs by young draftees.

Six months after landing in Vietnam, while on long range recon deep behind enemy territory, George received the "million dollar wound." Lt. George Ramos was part of a five-man Special Forces team assigned to gather intelligence near the Laotian-Cambodian border. The team broke camp and began to move quietly through thick jungle brush when they began to receive small arms fire. In an instant, the team was pinned down approximately 200 meters from the designated clearing for extraction.

The team radioed for air support. In approximately ten minutes, U.S. gunships hovered in and began suppressing the area with fire. During the brief firefight on the ground, Lt. James Holland received serious injuries to both legs after a mortar shell exploded close to him. The team fought their way through smoke and burning brush and made it to the perimeter of the landing zone.

George carried Lt. Holland on his back fifty meters to the center of the LZ as two choppers came in to extract the team. George helped position Lt. Holland safely in the first chopper and gave the pilot the hand signal to lift off. Instinctively George turned towards the brush and began firing to provide cover for the departing chopper. As the first chopper rose up and hovered above, George glanced up in time to observe the large number 23 painted under the chopper's base. He looked away towards the LZ perimeter, and was horrified as he witnessed a rocket propelled grenade slam into the first chopper. A bright fireball flashed, and then the thundering blast launched the mangled chopper into a spin into the jungle below, sending hot metal flying in all directions.

The last thing George remembered was a hot piercing object entering his left leg. Seriously wounded, George lost consciousness. His next recollection was waking from surgery in a naval hospital. After the surgery, the doctors claimed that "only God" was responsible for George keeping his leg. The military flew his wife to Japan, and she later accompanied George to the Veterans' Hospital in Phoenix, where she and their son were constant visitors.

While in the hospital, George wrote articles about the American flag, draft card burners, and draft dodgers that fled to Canada, Mexico, and other countries. In general, he wrote about people that opposed the war in Vietnam. In his articles, he opined that our elected leaders make the decision to go to war, whether right or wrong. By burning the American flag and draft cards, the war protestors were sending the wrong message, not only to the young men dying in Vietnam, but also to the whole world. In a democracy, we have the right to question decisions made by the government, but it should be done peacefully and diplomatically.

The Army was aware of George's articles, and that he had a few more months before his separation from the Army Reserves. His superiors advised him to discontinue writing the articles. In return, they would send him all over the nation as a representative of the United States Army, to spread his views to the public in person.

The Army wanted to see how draft-age young men would react to this veteran of two wars, a veteran who was seriously wounded in each of those wars. There were rumors that in the near future, the draft would be abolished for an all-volunteer army and they wanted to be ready to keep the numbers up.

George liked the idea very much. He enjoyed the tremendous exposure to the public. Jenny and his son traveled with him and saw parts of the country they had never seen before, all for free. Four months later, George returned to Arizona to finish his term as Senator.

By now, he had earned the respect of most of his peers and the wrath of a few. At the end of his second term, the Third Party's Presidential candidate approached him to be a speechwriter and adviser. Hamilton Langley's good friend, Mrs. Sommers, recommended George when she turned the job down. Things were moving fast for George now, and Mrs. Sommers wanted to get him all the national exposure she could. George accepted the position.

In Arizona, he was knows as a straight and honest Senator. He was also know for drafting and helping pass legislation to do away with "graft." That was the practice used by some politicians to enrich themselves in and out of politics. Arizona politicians were not the only ones using that practice. "Graft" was being used in many other states including the Federal Government.

Once again, George and Jenny were on the move. This time their destination was Baltimore, Maryland, the "Charm City," and the Presidential Campaign headquarters for the Third Party.

CHAPTER 9

▼

It was a challenge for George to work with Langley day after day, but he loved every minute of it. Now he traveled with Langley all over the country. The speeches George composed were brilliant. They were easy to understand and straight to the point. Langley dazzled the crowds everywhere he went. Sometimes George introduced Langley to the crowd, and that gave him a chance to warm up the audience, usually with a little humor. The people loved it.

One day as they prepared to address a huge crowd in Los Angeles, Langley temporarily lost his voice. There was concern for a moment, then George suggested that he do the speech himself. Langley thought it over for a while then agreed, "Why not? George wrote the speech and he is an excellent speaker."

George first apologized to the crowd for Langley's loss of voice. He continued, "To begin, I'm going to ask all of you to help me recite the Pledge of Allegiance to the flag." He faced the flag in front of him, and put his right hand over his heart and began to recite the Pledge. Langley noticed that George had not even started the speech, and he already had the crowd going. Before he was halfway through, George knew that he pushed the right buttons. He had the whole crowd helping him. George spoke in a very passionate and eloquent manner. When he was finished, the crowd went crazy and rewarded him with a standing ovation. Langley saw how well George handled himself, and the way the audience reacted to him. The electricity this young man could generate in people stunned him. He made a mental note of that. From that point on, they shared the speaking chores, until Langley's heart attack.

After they returned from a successful speaking engagement on the west coast, Langley and George were both excited and exhausted. Their non-stop travel schedule was starting to take its toll. A planned speech for 10,000 dockworkers resulted in an unexpected crowd of over 50,000 enthusiastic followers. The welcome they received was beyond their expectations. Local politicians and members of other political parties who noticed the snowballing effect to the Third Party, also wanted to get on the bandwagon.

As they planned the upcoming trip to Cleveland, Hamilton fell to the floor, gasping for air. He was short of breath and could not talk. George dropped the papers he was working on and knelt down beside his friend. He knew with one look that Hamilton was having a heart attack. George got up and went to the phone, called for an ambulance, and then went back to Hamilton and performed CPR on him. By the time the paramedics arrived, he had his friend breathing, thanks to the CPR training he received in the Army. For the time being, Hamilton was out of danger.

George stayed at the hospital with Hamilton's family all day and into the night. Late that evening, the doctor came in with the news. Langley had suffered a massive heart attack. There was some damage to his heart, but now he was asleep and stable. A crucial time was approaching, the doctor said. "I am not going to diminish your hopes or elevate them by any means, but if he can hang on for the next 36 hours, he will have a 50-50 chance of full recovery. We did all we could possibly do, now it's up to the man upstairs."

Early the next morning, as he drove to the hospital, George was alone with his thoughts. *If something does happen to Hamilton, what will happen to the party? Is the party doomed to fail if Hamilton's dies? There's no way Langley can continue. His health will prevent him from doing anything strenuous. God knows that a campaign for the presidency could kill him. And what about Dector Jimenes? Can he rise to the occasion? Will he buckle under the pressure? Dector Jimenes is a brilliant lawyer. With his political knowledge, law savvy, and good looks, he's made an astounding contribution to the party.* George continued his thoughts. *Yes, Jimenes is the man to take Langley's place.* He still wondered what kind of answers there were as he arrived at the hospital.

George headed directly to the intensive care unit. Hamilton's family met him in the hallway and told him that Hamilton was conscious, in good spirits.

In ICU, the nurses strictly enforced the "one at a time" rule for visitors. Hamilton's son was keeping vigil with his father as George walked in.

"He has been waiting for you, Mr. Ramos," he said quietly as he left the two men alone.

George nodded and walked up to the bed. *God, he looks bad.* He knew well that you always try to cheer up the patient. "I see you're looking better. You will be out of here very soon." He hated to lie. There was no way this man would ever see the outside of this hospital again. George had seen the very same look on Army buddies and other soldiers in Korea, and once you see that look you never forget it.

Hamilton knew that George was lying but silently forgave him. He knew that his time was near. It was uncanny, but true. He would probably say the same thing if it was the other way around. After the usual petty talk, Hamilton changed his tone of voice and there was a serious look in his eyes.

"George, I want you to listen to me and please don't interrupt me. I feel that it is my duty to the party, and by the same token, to the American people to make this announcement." George knew exactly what was coming. "I know that this is not the place or the time, but there isn't much time." He then produced an envelope. "These are written instructions to our party's nominating committee concerning my substitution after my departure to be administered legally according to federal and state regulations. You are my choice, George. You will lead the party to victory."

George was about to say something, but stopped as Hamilton gestured with his hand as he continued. "Our country is ready for the change we have been preaching. The party, under your leadership, will make that change a reality. The people want very much to see it. They are waiting out there, ready to fight for it with the best weapon known to democracy, their vote." George just stood there not knowing what to say as Hamilton went on. "As a Mexican-American, it will be the toughest fight anybody running for President has ever faced, but in the end, you will succeed. With the Third Party's victory, America will be a better place for all the people. Your victory will prove to the whole world that ours is a true democracy. Now it is all in your hands. Go and do your job. I wish you lots and lots of luck. You are going to need it."

They looked at each other for a few seconds, then George asked, "What about Jimenes?"

Hamilton replied, "Jimenes is very necessary to the party. There is no other man that knows political law as he does. Even you, with a degree in Law and Political Science, have to agree with me. Anyway, he suggested that himself. He will be your running mate as he was for me."

One of the doctors came into the room and told George that Mr. Hamilton needed to rest now. George moved closer to the bed, and holding back the tears, shook hands with his friend. George knew well that this was the last time he would ever see his friend alive. They held hands for a moment as Hamilton said with a weak smile, "Good luck and God bless you." George slowly turned and walked out of the room.

Hamilton's death was a dramatic event and the media played it as such. They bombarded the American public with negative articles such as, *THE RISE AND FALL OF THE THIRD PARTY, LEADING PARTY IS DOOMED TO FAIL,* and *SO MUCH FOR CHANGE.* However, George could not blame them, there was so little time left before the election, six months to be exact.

The media did not realize that the Third Party was for real. Their strength was not limited to one candidate alone, even though Hamilton was one of the best. Every individual member of the party equally shared their agenda, their beliefs, and convictions. They also knew that adversity brought an equal or a better benefit. The Third Party strongly believed that change was inevitable and they would fight to the bitter end to achieve it. *PERSEVERE* was their slogan. The media also did not count on the American public, the masses who now realized that change in this country was evident and very much needed. The public was willing to go with whoever was ready to lead them. Yes, the Third Party was on the right track. A new candidate would be chosen to lead them on to victory and they did not have to go very far to find one.

Dector Mcfarland Jimenes, Langley's running mate, had a discussion with Hamilton Langley three days before Langley died. Dector agreed to what Langley asked of him. As soon as Langley's death was announced, Jimenes called a meeting at the Third Party Headquarters in Baltimore. Now he had to get the others to agree with Langley's request. Jimenes asked for a minute of silence in honor of Langley. As the meeting began, George was nervous because he knew what was coming and he had not yet decided what to do.

Jimenes first said a few words for their fallen leader. He continued, "We haven't much time to decide who will be running for President in Langley's place for the Third Party. I had a long talk with Langley before he died and he suggested that George Ramos would make the best choice, and I agreed with him." He waited a little while, and then said, "If you are wondering about me, forget it. I turned it down and I have my reasons, and Hamilton agreed with me. You have two hours to decide, and remember it has to be a majority vote."

After one hour, they came back. "It's unanimous for George Ramos."

"Thank you," Jimenes said, "Now we have work to do and not much time to do it." Jimenes approached George and asked, "Are you up to the challenge?" George just stared at him. Jimenes was well aware of the monumental task George would face, but it was their only chance. He knew the answer.

On the way home, George thought about the events of the day. He knew that as a political speechwriter and a public speaker, he ranked up there with the best of them. His political career had flourished faster than he had anticipated.

After leading in most of the polls, Hamilton Langley was dead. In the event of his death, Langley had instructed the party to nominate George Ramos as his substitute. The party unanimously approved the request, and chose George to take Hamilton's place. George truly believed that the Third Party's agenda was the best thing going for the American people. In his mind, he knew that America was ready for change, but America was not ready for a Mexican-American President. The timing was all wrong. He believed that the nation would elect a woman President first, and then perhaps they would choose an African-American as President. Maybe, sometime in the future, a Mexican-American might have a fair chance to become the President of the United States. Winning the election now, however, would be an enormous task.

George had enough confidence in himself to handle the job. He had to admit, he actually felt good about it. George knew that if by chance the people elected him President of the United States, he would become the most powerful man in the world.

If Hamilton's death was the catalyst that added fuel to the newspaper articles in a rather surprising election, the Third Party's choice for a substitute candidate was an even bigger shocker. It was hot enough to burn the keys on a reporter's typewriter. That is what a journalist's dreams are all about.

The first story that broke after the announcement was made read like a soap opera. "Third Party survives after the death of their candidate, only to commit political suicide by choosing a Mexican to take his place." Another article read, "Third Party digs a second burial hole within a week," referring to their choice of candidate.

The opposition was stunned, but was now relieved that the party leading in all polls in the country, would not be a factor in the coming election. Soon the jokes began to surface. The incumbent President could hardly keep from laughing when he read an article in a magazine that read, "Third Party solicits help from the Burrito Brothers in their run for the border (Presidential election). What will they think of next, the Federales?" The late night talk shows referred to the Third Party's Presidential and Vice Presidential candidates as the "Tacos for Lunch Bunch."

What they didn't know was that Ramos was Mexican but Jimenes was not. He was born Dector Mcfarland in Chicago, Illinois. His father, a wealthy real estate broker, died when Dector was just a baby. When Dector was two years old, his mother decided to move west. They settled in the San Fernando Valley of the Los Angeles area. There she met and married another wealthy real estate broker, Jaime "Jim" Jimenes. Thus, his name was changed to Dector Jimenes.

When Hamilton Langley passed away and the party chose Ramos to take his place, congratulations arrived from different parts of the nation. The very first one was a telephone call from George's mentor, Mrs. Sommers. She was so exited that she almost cried when she told him how happy she was for him. They talked some and then she said, "I heard that you had trouble deciding whether to run for the job. Why was that?"

"I thought that I wasn't ready, that I needed more experience. But the most important thing was that I don't believe the nation is ready for a Mexican-American President."

"You may be right, but in this world there is a reason for everything that happens. It is your destiny. You have the qualities, regardless of your experience, and most of all, real leaders are not made. They are born. You are a born leader."

"God help me," George said, more to himself than anybody else.

"Go then, and realize your childhood dream. Go with these thoughts in your head—honesty, integrity, truth, and love for country. All of us in Clarkston love you, and we will be behind you all the way." When he hung up the phone, George sat there and stared at the phone for a long time.

Three weeks later, George received a phone call from Neil Sommers. It was bad news. Mrs. Sommers had suffered a stroke and was in a Phoenix hospital in critical condition. George and Jenny immediately flew to Phoenix. Mr. Sommers met them in intensive care. George noticed that Neil had tears in his eyes and asked him, "How is she doing?"

"She's paralyzed on her whole left side. She is conscious and she can hear, but she can't see or talk. Do you want to see her?" George just nodded.

George and Neil went in and stood by the bed. What George saw was the frail wasted body of the woman he remembered as a strong, athletic lady, that always had a smile on her face. She was like a mother to George and he loved her as such.

"Honey. Honey," Neil said in a soft voice, "George is here to see you." He wanted to continue but he couldn't as he moved back. George knelt down by the bed, held one of her hands, and said, "I'm here, Mrs. Sommers. I'll always be here for you as you were for me most of my life." George saw tears running down her cheeks and he started sobbing like a kid. He couldn't help it.

He held her cold hand for a while, then he felt her hand get colder and he understood what was happening. He looked at Neil as he slowly moved his head from side to side. Neil moved to the other side of the bed, knelt down and grabbed her other hand as both were now sobbing. As she died, they both saw the sweet smile that was her trait, and even though she was paralyzed on one side they both felt her hands squeeze theirs at the same time.

As George and Jenny flew back to Maryland, he looked out of the window and again saw the sweet smile on Mrs. Sommers' face, an image that he would never forget as long as he lived.

CHAPTER 10

▼

The road to the presidency of the United States was full of stops, detours, potholes and dangerous curves for George, and he knew it. He was very realistic. He was resilient and believed in what he was doing. He loved his country and if he could legally do anything to make this nation a better place for every citizen, he would. Unknown to George Ramos, there was an individual that was very intent on preventing him from reaching that goal.

Senator Karl Graves was the son of a World War II German ace pilot. Karl Erich Graves Sr. served with Germany's Luftwaffe during World War II. Shooting down over three hundred planes, Graves Sr. was awarded the famed Knights Cross of the Iron Cross. During the battle of Kursk, Graves Sr. was shot down and captured by the U.S. allies. He was imprisoned in the Soviet Union and eventually extradited to a U.S. concentration camp. After his wife perished in a U.S. air raid in Germany, his young son Karl Jr. was sent to live with his grandmother near Hamburg. After the war, Karl's father refused repatriation. The U.S. Government, well aware of his flying skills, offered him a job as a test pilot for the Air Force. He brought his son to America, and after a year on the job, married an American woman, and thus became a naturalized American citizen.

The death of Karl Sr. in a flying accident left a widow and a young boy alone but in excellent financial condition. In addition, the Air Force promised a full scholarship for Karl Jr. at any school of his choice. After high school, he chose Boston College, where he graduated at the top of his class with a major in Political Science.

In college, he became obsessed with the power that was manifested by the Nazi Party before World War II. He read anything he could find on Hitler and the Nazi movement. By the time he finished school, he transformed himself into a racist—a white supremacist—a secret he kept well guarded. His dream since high school was to become a powerful world leader. He strongly believed that it was leadership that was responsible for the fall of empires of the past. Most emperors or leaders did not have qualities that it takes to dominate the world. But he had a master plan. First, he would become a great politician. As he honed his political career, he would unite all the white supremacist groups and individuals in the country and become their leader, all at the same time. So far, his plan was ahead of schedule by his timetable. He was now a U.S. Senator and Grand Wizard of the feared Ku Klux Klan. That was the first phase of the plan. He had become a brilliant master of politics, an impressive thinker, and visionary. Others said that he was very ambitious and arrogant—a manipulator who always used people for his own gain. Some even thought that the Senator was psychotic but wouldn't dare say it. Yet his political career flourished and he moved up the political ladder at a very fast pace.

In Washington, Senator Graves was well respected for his political prowess, but he was also feared and hated by many. He was nobody's fool and was well aware of the fear and hatred, but it didn't make a bit of difference to him. He just shrugged it off and said to himself, "Fuckum," his favorite word for those that did not approve of him. According to his plan, in four more years, he would be President. He would then deal with the unwanted garbage in Washington, the second part of his plan.

Everything was working the way he had planned. The next task was to unite all of the white supremacist groups into one strong group. He was already the KKK's most trusted leader, but there were groups out there that had to be contacted. His plan was to have all supremacist groups under his command. That took him a long time because it was all done secretly. He finally succeeded but it had not been easy.

Senator Graves thought of the first meeting that he called of all white supremacist groups in the nation. The meeting took place in a very secluded area somewhere in Georgia. He had no idea what he was getting into. The first to show up were the scum, hardcore racists, and boisterous smart-asses, ignorant of the importance related to the assemblage. Some carried six packs of beer. A few were way past the state of sobriety and most were armed. This was an array of people with traditional costumes of their respective organizations.

The Senator watched the parade of clowns and ruffians wandering about. *How are we ever going to educate this bunch of goofy bastards to be solid citizens of a white-only nation?* He wanted to vomit, but he was responsible for this den of inequity.

He pretended to ignore this performance of totally unacceptable behavior, and daydreamed of the final domination of the races. *Funny. Here I am in deep shit that could ruin my plan and career, madder then a son of a bitch, and thinking of dominating the non-white race. Whenever I do this, it is like a drug to me, an upper. It makes me hallucinate with my eyes open. In my physical insensibility I see the 'bean eaters' working for peanuts. I see some that the nation has made into sports heroes. I see them working in plantations of an all white America. The ones portrayed as martial arts experts are actually meek and will be easy to control. But the fighters, yes the real fighters will be the toughest to dominate. But alas, they have been burned once and they will be burned again, and this time there will be a real Holocaust."*

He gathered his senses and came back to reality, and what he deemed the superior and intellectual side of his brain began to function. *I have to play it cool. I must learn to control my emotions.* He remembered that as a kid he would lose his temper easily. As he grew up he did a better job of controlling it. Nevertheless, the problem was still there and he understood that some day that type of behavior would get him in trouble—real trouble.

He walked to the center of the circle created by the leaders of each group, and the chaotic demonstrations of insolent bravado began to subside. He raised his hand in the universal salute of friendship. The light from the flickering tongues of fire leaped from the big logs in the campfire. The silence now became intense as he began.

"Brothers, the march to an all white nation starts tonight. The time to mend our differences between groups is here. As separate groups we are pissing against the wind in a losing battle. As a unit we will be stronger and will function more efficiently. We have to do it the smart way. Let us put the guns away for now. By joining organizations, becoming more active in politics, and infiltrating law enforcement, we will beat the system from the inside. Keep the guns clean and close by and when the time comes for their necessity we will be ready." He went on to explain the plan and procedure. He ended his speech by saying, "What has been said here stays here."

*   *   *   *

When Hamilton Langley passed away and the Third Party replaced him with George Ramos, the incumbent President relaxed and smiled more often. He even threw a party at his 120-acre retreat for his advisers and close friends. In a toast he declared, "Let's do it one more time. To the next four years." Everybody laughed and the gloating was on.

Two weeks later, his advisers told that he was behind in the polls again. He began to yell. "What in the world is wrong with the American public? A damn greaser runs for President and he is ahead of me in the polls? He claims that America needs a change? Well let me tell you what is going to happen. If he wins this election, the only change the American public is going to get is changing their eating habits from ham and eggs to tortillas and beans, stupid bastards." He threw his hands up and walked out of the room.

When the Third Party lost Langley, a native of Georgia, the polls began to change in favor of the other two parties. The Third Party knew they had work to do there and time was running out. George went to the southern states with his unmatched charisma, truth, sincerity, and above all, a convincing agenda. George began unleashing a barrage of fiery speeches that would mesmerize the crowds. But what the voters seemed to appreciate most, was the way he would initiate his speeches. He would always lead the audience with the Pledge of Allegiance to the flag.

George seemed to have it all—good looks, unmistakable charm, and wit that had not been seen since the days of President John F Kennedy. His record of accomplishment as an Arizona Senator preceded him as a champion for minorities and labor. Veterans proudly stood behind the decorated war hero, as he pledged to never forget their plight in the mired abyss of red tape that continued to plague them in obtaining recognition and benefits.

Nothing seemed to be working for the incumbent President. Then Senator Graves hit on the idea of an investigation of the Third Party's candidate based on some ugly rumors he fabricated. *Why not?* Approval from the Congressional Committee, of which he was chairman, would come fast and easy. The President, knowing well that he was losing the election, jumped at the idea, even at the protest of his advisers. The President was convinced that what the Senator was doing was one of those, 'I'll scratch your back, and you scratch mine' deals that continuously go on in Capitol Hill and the hell with the public. He was concerned that time was running out and he had to do whatever was necessary to win the presidency once again. The President was positive that the Senator was trying to use him, as he used everyone else around him for his own benefit. He didn't care, because this time the benefit would be mutual.

Senator Graves began a series of allegations and investigations against the Third Party's candidate. The allegations were untrue, and the investigations were nothing but witch hunts, but that didn't stop the Senator. The idea was to have the media spread the false rumors all over the nation, and thus plant doubts and mistrust in the voters' minds before the election. The Senator justified his actions to himself. *This sort of strategy is lowdown and dirty, but it works. This is nothing new. It has been done since day one. Sure the rumormongers take some heat, but after your party wins the election, who gives a shit? Who cares whether the loser was a homosexual, a woman beater, a drunk, or whether he smoked pot? Nobody will care.*

In the meantime, two private investigators who worked for Senator Graves returned to Washington to report some very good news, according to them. When they arrived in the Senator's office, the Senator said. "This had better be good. You people are getting good money so I don't want any bullshit."

One of the investigators closed the door as the other began to whisper, as if someone else was listening. "We went to Clarkston and talked to a lot of people. We checked at the hospital where the subject was allegedly born and everything seemed to be in order."

"I don't want to know what you didn't find. I want to know what you found, damn it."

"I'm getting to it. We decided to go to Mexico to a small town not too far from the border. We asked a few questions, and found a man that was familiar with the birth of a baby from a couple from Clarkston. The date of the birth he gave us is the same day that Mr. Ramos was born."

"That doesn't tell me anything," the Senator said, clearly irritated.

"Well, Sir, the birth happened on the Mexican side of the border and not on the American side."

Then the Senator asked, "Are you sure?" Now he was very interested.

"Check it out yourself," the man said, and passed an envelope to the Senator. He continued, "There are times, dates, and all the details you need."

The Senator looked at the papers when one of the men said, "There is one more thing, Sir."

"And what is that?" the Senator asked.

"He wants $5,000 dollars to verify that information." The Senator was silent for a moment. It was the first time somebody tried to extort him. Usually he was the one doing the honors. What really pissed him off was the fact that it was a stupid peon doing the extortion, and furthermore, there was nothing he could do about it. He needed the verification.

The Senator finally spoke up. "Okay, I'll write him a check, and…"

He was about to finish when he was interrupted. "He doesn't want any checks, IOUs, or promises. He wants cash," one of the men said.

"That dirty bastard." Senator Graves was looking for a way to outsmart the peon, and finally said, "I'll give you the $5,000 he wants. You guys go down there and give it to him, and tell him that there is another $2,000 if he comes over here and tells the press what he told you."

The deal was made and the peon said that he would be there if they needed him. A week later, some reporters in Sonoyta, Mexico began to ask questions. They found one man that knew the person they were looking for. When they asked him where the man was at, he answered, "Oh, si, Manuel he got mucho monee and he go."

"Where did he go, this Manuel?"

"Quien sabe. Who knows? Manuel mucho loco. Maybe Guadalajara, maybe Mexico City or Acapulco. Who knows what loco Manuel does?"

So much for verification.

Senator Graves was elated with the report his two investigators brought him. What he needed most now was verification. His plan was to get the peon to come to the United States and talk to the news people. After he verified the birth, the Senator would make him disappear without paying the rest of the money.

When he found out that the peon had flown the coop, he went berserk. He was used to getting the upper hand on any deal. He was so angry that he decided to turn the information to the media regardless of verification.

Later in his office, the Senator tried to decide what to do next. He knew that a victory by the Third Party would certainly ruin the timetable for his plan. "Okay," the Senator said, "because time is short, I will play my last card. I cannot let the Mex ruin my plans." He went to the phone, made a call, and then walked out of his office.

The Senator hated the President with a passion, but he needed him on record for what he had in mind. It was a precaution. Just in case he went down, he would take the President with him. The President said on the phone, "You do whatever you have to do and this time do it right." The President thought that the Senator was going to plant some more dirt on Ramos. Smiling, he hung up the phone. That was all that the Senator needed. He had approval from the President on a recorded message.

In the end, the investigation failed to implicate any wrongdoing by Ramos. There was no stopping the Third Party now. Senator Graves decided that, unknown to anybody else, he would stop Ramos and the Third Party. He had a plan, a reckless and dangerous plan. Nevertheless, it had to be carried out. He was well aware of the consequences of failure but he was desperate. Before he got off the plane in Mobile, Alabama, the Senator thought of the considerable risk in the adventure he was about to take. *I must not fail. I will not fail. The future of our country depends on it.* Now, he didn't care. There was no other way.

He rented a van at the airport, and headed out to the predetermined place he had carefully selected. The abandoned Boy Scout camp had ten acres of fenced-in wooded area. There was only one gate that guarded the road to the campsite at the center of the property. The property was previously acquired by a close friend of the Senator in a trade for a piece of property in the city. It was an ideal place for the clandestine meeting he had in mind. The Senator was extremely careful of the meeting places he selected. He also protected his identity with extreme caution. He always wore the hood at these meetings. There were only three people that knew who he was.

The Senator was excited with anticipation as he drove into the camp. In the camp, there was a large semicircle of sitting benches made of logs and stones. In front of the semicircle there was a throne-like seat made of the same material. He parked the van behind the throne. He took off his coat and slipped on his purple and white robe with yellow trim, denoting the highest rank in the organization. To complete his transformation from a prominent politician to a feared white supremacist, he covered his head with a long pointed hood. Some equated the hood with the horn of the devil to instill fear in the hearts of those that dared to oppose them.

He walked to the center of the semicircle and lit the logs that were prepared by his friend. He then walked back to the throne and sat down to wait. He had come two hours early. He had plenty of time to think.

As the light of the fire flickered with the night breeze, the man sitting on the throne made a spectacular figure. From behind, he could have been mistaken for the Pope, contemplating the salvation of the world in a silent prayer. But it was the front view that truly identified what this sinister figure represented. The hood only showed the two gleaming eyes of a violent individual who had sunk to the depths of racial hatred and bigotry, to embrace the corrupt evil ideologies of his organization.

As the Senator waited, his thoughts wandered to the days when the Third Party lost Hamilton Langley and announced their substitute candidate. He, like everyone else, thought that the Third Party's dream of victory was going down the drain, even though they lead in all the polls. He couldn't have been more wrong. If polls are the instrument by which political elections are measured, the Third Party was well on the road to victory. To say that the Senator was worried was an understatement. *The time has come to do what we should have done in the first place.* The leaders of the other organizations began to arrive.

This meeting was serious and only for the leaders. They concluded that time was short, and in order to stop the Third Party from winning the election, they needed to do away with the Third Party's candidate. All of them agreed. All that was needed was the method and who was going to take care of it. The Senator already had a plan. It didn't take long for the rest to agree that the Senator would arrange everything at a cost of $250,000. At first, some thought that the amount was very high, but soon were convinced that so was the risk.

The Senator's job was to contract the best hitman that money could buy. Through some shadowy people he knew in Europe, the Senator found Karlos. Karlos was the best in the world for that type of business—also the most expensive for that matter. As usual, the money would be deposited in a bank in Switzerland under a fictitious name. The time would be before the election. The place and method was always left to the perpetrator.

CHAPTER 11

▼

He heard the heavy footsteps long before the big door finally opened. William Perkins stood up as the group entered the room. The President was followed by the Vice President, two Secret Service officers, and a tall well built man that walked with a slight limp. The man limped because of a wound he received many years ago as a rookie FBI agent, during a gun battle with a fugitive from the law. For some unknown reason, Bert Goodman was also there.

Bert was the President's childhood best friend, next-door neighbor, and room-mate in college. Only after college had they gone their separate ways to pursue their illustrious careers. Three years ago, Bert Goodman brilliantly ran the campaign for his friend. They ran away with the election for two reasons—the shrewd and excellent handling of the campaign by Bert and the solid political knowledge of his friend. Some people said that the insane thirst for power by the incumbent President also had very much to do with his election.

Now they were challenged by a very different situation. To start, the man was a virtually unknown Third Party candidate who had held only one political office and that office was only a state level position. But this man had the masses behind him, and now many special interest groups, such as the mining industry, NRA, labor unions, and ethnic groups were behind him as well. Money and sure votes were coming in by the thousands. Yes, he was a formidable threat all right, but it wasn't over yet. There was one thing in the incumbent President's favor. Their adversary was a Mexican, and they planned to crucify him.

The President knew that it was important to have the two agents at his side at all times, but it was hard to get used to it. At times, it seemed that he had no privacy at all. The tall man looked at Perkins, and as their eyes met, each knew that there was no need for further acknowledgment. They had known each other for many years. They were best of friends, and Buttler limped because he had taken a bullet meant for Perkins. Bill had never forgotten it. As officers of the law, they had gone their separate ways. Tom was head of the FBI in Maryland and Bill was head of the Secret Service in Washington.

Perkins was not sure how the President would take the new information that was inside the brown folder he clutched in his sweaty hands. He knew that the President was unpredictable as hell. *Why am I nervous?* Was it because the information they came across just by luck after one year, may or may not be important to the President? He knew that it was not lack of efficiency on his part, for he proved time and again that he was the best head of the Secret Service they've had in many years. Neither was the fact that he had one more year to go to retirement and wanted to go out on a positive note. No, it was something else, something that was very much related to what was going on now, but he could not put his finger on it. He felt that whatever it was, it had to be important and time was running out.

The President walked over to the big leather chair behind the oak desk and sat down. Perkins looked at the group as his eyes came to rest on the Vice President. There he was with that phony smile that manifested more contempt than pleasure or amusement. *That man, if you can call him that, is the perfect example of an asshole—completely useless.* Perkins was an excellent judge of character and the first time they met, he decided that the man was an arrogant bastard, and in time, that man could turn into a real asshole. It wasn't long before he was proven correct. They disagreed as to how an investigation was proceeding. The Vice President said the department was incompetent. He called the agents a collection of glorified gumshoes when he heard that the man they were investigating turned up clean. He even suggested planting some dirt on the man so they could use it during the campaign. Perkins was a man of integrity and was not about to play dirty pool for anybody, even if his job depended on it.

The President sensed that Perkins was hesitant because of the group, and spoke up. "It is okay, Bill. We are all in this together. Tell us what was so important that you could not tell me over the phone."

"Very well, Sir," said Perkins, as he fumbled with the brown folder. He produced a piece of paper and began to read. "One George Ramos was born in the back seat of an automobile on the way to the hospital. He was not born at the Clarkston hospital in Arizona as the birth certificate states. The father, a natural-born American citizen, was a mining engineer for the Southern Arizona Copper Company. At the time of the birth, the father was working at a mine in

Mexico, close to the United States border. The company rented a house for Ramos and his wife in Mexico, three miles from the mine, and they would go back to Clarkston only on weekends. He was born on a Tuesday night." There was silence for a few seconds but it seemed like an eternity. The Vice President broke the short silence and almost laughing said, "What is so important about that?"

He was about to continue when the President interrupted. He looked at Perkins' dark blue eyes and asked, "Are you suggesting…" He never finished.

"Exactly, Sir, and very possible." All eyes were on Perkins now, especially the ones on the inquisitive look on the face of the Vice President.

The President continued, "That is something worth looking into."

"It's a long shot, too many years in between, but there is always a slim chance." Perkins answers were more relaxed now. In his profession, he quickly learned never to assume anything. He must be sure. The others in the group, except for the tall man, still looked puzzled as Perkins continued. "There is one more thing, Sir."

The President stood up. "And?" he asked.

Perkins looked not at the President but directly at Buttler and said, "There is word out on the street that a contract has been put out on our man." There was dead silence this time.

Before the importance of the statement sank in, the Vice President triumphantly concluded, "Well, that solves our problem, huh?"

Perkins thought, "Why does the President keep this idiot around?"

The President, obviously annoyed at his Vice President, asked, "Do we know who wants him dead?"

"No, but we are working on it. We do know that it is definitely a go and whoever is paying wants him real bad. $250,000 worth," Perkins answered.

Goodman thought only of the campaign, and finally spoke up. "No! There is no way we can let that happen. Any assassination attempt, especially if it fails, could be disastrous to our campaign." Everybody looked at Goodman. They saw a very serious face, as perspiration ran down his forehead to his eyebrows. His coke bottle glasses were almost down to his nose. With two fingers, he pushed his glasses up in their place and continued, "Don't you see? There are rumors already out there that we will go to any lengths to keep that man from becoming President. If we are to have a chance at winning, we must try to prevent the assassination attempt."

They had to agree with Goodman. They could not afford another scandal before the elections. Besides, if Perkins was able to prove his hunch correct, the

President was sure to win the election. The meeting ended with the announcement that the FBI had been brought in to assist the Secret Service.

On the way to the office, Perkins thought of the sensible decision made today. *It's bad enough to hear about political assassinations in other countries, but here in my own domain? Not on my watch.* One thing for sure though, he felt good about being in a position to keep it from happening in this country. That was part of his job and he knew he was good at it.

At the office, he went directly to a file cabinet and pulled out a folder. As he headed for his desk, the phone rang. "It never fails." It was more of a thought than a statement. He grabbed the phone and sat down in the black leather chair. "Yes," he answered. It was the sweet voice of Morina, his secretary. He highly admired her efficiency, hard work habits, and neatness, but her voice was a tribute to her age. The woman was sixty years old, and she still had the voice of a teenage girl.

"Mr. Thomas Buttler to see you, Sir," he heard Morina say.

Without hesitating Perkins answered, "Send him in, Morina, and thank you."

Perkins was beginning to sympathize with the man he was to protect from being assassinated. He wondered about this man. History taught him that men like him are rare and unique. They appear on this world once in a lifetime. They are tough and straight as an arrow. They are usually sensitive to the needs of the masses, the poor, the underdog, and the oppressed. Some perform great deeds and manage to save entire nations. Others never finish their work, but the foundations they have established will remain throughout the history of mankind.

This man had managed to touch the lives of almost everybody in this country. His name was a household word. Was it the way he could speak to the people? Could it be his charisma? Or was it the simple truth in his speeches that made the people admire him? Whatever it was, this man rose from obscurity to challenge for the presidency of the United States.

Perkins had a gut feeling that the time was right for someone like this man to emerge. You did not have to be too smart to see what was happening in our country. He thought of the way Congress voted down the increase of the minimum wage from $2.00 to $2.75 an hour. Then they approved a thirty percent raise for themselves. They reasoned that they couldn't send their kids to college on $50,000 a year salary.

The economy was bad, the rich were getting richer, and the poor were getting poorer. Yes, even Perkins believed that the time for change was here.

CHAPTER 12

▼

Buttler wanted to discuss protection strategy for the Third Party's candidate with Perkins, but something else was bothering him. As Morina, Perkins' secretary, led him to Perkins' office, Buttler said to her, "Morina, you are like a breath of fresh air. Don't ever change." She just smiled, showing her beautiful white teeth and walked away. Buttler had known her for many years. Buttler was about to knock when he heard Perkins' voice.

"Come on in, Tom. I am glad we have a chance to work together again. I will really appreciate any help you can give me." Buttler limped to the leather sofa and sat down, and turned his head away from Perkins. Perkins continued to talk. "Something is bothering you, isn't it? I know you too well. What's on your mind, partner?"

Buttler finally looked at Perkins and said, "I know that protection for a Third Party candidate is usually a matter of formality unless that person is a threat to win the election. As far as I can remember, that has never happened before. Now I believe that this time we will have our hands full."

"I realize that, but that is not what is really bothering you. Is it?"

"Not exactly," Tom answered looking towards the window again.

"Well, what is it? It always helps to talk about it."

He stood up and limped to the front of the desk. He faced Bill, and said, "Karlos the Jackal." This time he showed real concern on his face. There was a short silence as both men looked at each other. Tom broke the stare first and walked to the window, then he turned around and faced Bill. "Look, we both heard that Karlos was killed in Algeria. The French don't think it was him, and there are rumors that he has been seen somewhere in Morocco. And...."

Before he finished talking, Perkins interrupted him. "What does that have to do with you worrying about it? There is something else isn't there?"

"Yes, I believe there is."

Perkins noticed a little excitement in Tom's voice and thought, "This has to be good. Tom doesn't get excited very easy."

"Do you remember the information we received from Interpol about the man that the French authorities said was working with Karlos? A young American, I believe."

"Yes, of course," Perkins answered in a low tone as he began to think.

"Do you have the file handy?" Tom asked.

Perkins moved to the file cabinet in the corner of the room. He looked through the files and selected a folder. He walked to his desk, passed the folder to Tom, and said, "There isn't much there."

Tom began to rifle through the papers immediately. As soon as he found a copy of a newspaper clipping, he announced, "This is all I need."

"You've seen that picture before," Perkins said with a bewildered look in his eyes.

"I know. I just wanted to make sure." Tom looked at the picture for a minute or two in silence, then pointed at it furiously. He declared, "It's him! By God, it's him!"

"What the hell are you talking about?" This time it was Perkins who was excited.

"I saw this same man at a supermarket a week ago. I know that the picture's quality is not that good, but that's him. At first it did not register in my head, but after your announcement concerning the contract on our man, it began to make a lot of sense."

"Are you absolutely sure?" He knew that was an unnecessary question. Tom was one of the best law enforcement officers that Bill had ever known.

Buttler still continued to look at the picture, and said, "It's not only that. I have a gut feeling on this one."

Perkins knew exactly how Tom felt. A month ago, there had been an assassination of a political figure in Montreal, Canada. The 'MO' on the assassination was very similar to that of Karlos the Jackal, according to Interpol. Since Karlos had never operated in that area, and Karlos had been dormant for more then two years, Perkins had put it out of his mind. Then there was the warning of a possible attempt on the Third Party's candidate. It gave him the feeling on his neck he always got when there was something important he had to know, but could not put his finger on what it was. Suddenly he got up, grabbed his coat, and faced Tom. "We don't have much time. Let's go pay a visit to Mr. Ramos."

"What about the investigation?" Tom asked.

"The hell with the investigation. You know as well as I do that the investigation is nothing but a witch hunt, and my job is national security. That means I protect the American citizens. One of those citizens is running for President and an assassin is threatening his life. I am not going to let it happen," he said in a serious voice.

"Are you thinking what I'm thinking?" Tom questioned, as he moved to the door.

Bill turned immediately towards Tom and simply gave a nod of agreement. "Our priority is now the protection of Presidential candidates and that has always been a hassle. But now, with all those crazy bastards out there trying to make a name for themselves, we have a professional to contend with. Like I said, we haven't much time."

George Ramos was under protection as a Presidential candidate and had never met Perkins or Buttler. There was a reason why they had never met. Protection for the Republican and Democratic Presidential candidates was always serious business, but whenever there was a third party, protection for their candidate was merely a formality. That protection was usually left to city police departments or personal bodyguards. This time, the incumbent President, under the direction of his advisers, decided that federal protection would serve two purposes. First, it would look good to the American public, and second, being close to the man would be beneficial for the investigation.

When Bill and Tom arrived at Ramos' residence, they saw a city police cruiser parked down the block from the house. Bill and Tom expected some type of a movement from the officers, but they kept drinking their coffee and eating their donuts and paid no attention to them. *So much for city protection.*

After the introductions, Mr. Ramos asked, "What can I do for you gentlemen?"

Bill and Tom looked at each other, but Perkins answered. "Mr. Ramos, we have reason to believe that there is going to be an assassination attempt on your life. Your life is in great danger."

Both men watched George's face to see what kind of a reaction he was going to have. There wasn't any. Then George spoke up. "Gentlemen, I do not want to give you the impression that I am naïve or ignorant, but what else is new? I mean, doesn't this sort of thing happen in every Presidential election?"

"Well, sure. In every Presidential election there is always some nut that believes in his own twisted mind this is the thing to do. This time, it is the real thing. We believe that a professional assassin has been hired to do the job. As of now, we are only speculating as to his identity, but there are no real facts. We are absolutely sure that there is going to be an attempt on your life," Perkins said.

"Assuming that what you say is true, and it is probably true, or you gentlemen would not be here, what am I supposed to do? Remember, fellows, that I am supposed to be running for President. I have to speak in public, attend countless meetings, travel all over the nation, and most of all I have to be seen by the people. If I have to go underground because some paid assassin is out there trying to do away with my life, then I have no business running for President of this great country. It goes with the job. You gentlemen understand this very well."

"We understand, and we agree with you, Mr. Ramos. We just wanted to warn you, and tell you that our people are going to be close, no matter where you go. Also, we need a schedule of your movements, and an assurance from you that you will let us know if you make any change in your schedule, no matter how small," Tom explained.

"I appreciate your concern, gentlemen. I will do my best." Then he turned to see where his wife and son were, and said, "Please keep this to yourselves."

"There is one more thing," Perkins said. "Will you wear this every time you go out?"

George looked at the tan bulletproof vest, and answered, "My favorite color."

On their way to the office, Perkins asked Tom, "What do you think of Mr. Ramos?"

"As a person, I find him very warm and charismatic. As a politician, I believe that he would make a good President. But as for winning, and I am merely stating a simple fact, I believe that the timing is wrong, and consequently, would make our jobs a lot tougher," Tom replied.

Perkins was silent for a while, then he said, "My sentiments exactly. I'm just wondering how he feels about it. He must have known the enormous odds that he would have to face, before he decided to run for President."

"The way I heard it, it was Langley's untimely death that put Mr. Ramos on the spot to do something he was not planning on."

"What makes you say that?"

"Well, according to the Washington Post, it was Langley, on his deathbed, who asked Ramos to take his place and run for President. He knew that he was not going to make it out of that hospital. You see, when Langley first met Ramos, he found out right away that they were both on the same page as to the needs of the American people. Then when he lost his voice and Ramos was delivering the speeches Ramos himself wrote, Langley noticed the magnetic nature he had with the American public, that they loved him. He represented a refreshing change to the people of America."

"He has shown intestinal fortitude and intelligence. I would feel terrible if anything was to happen to him," Perkins said, before he changed the subject.

"How about that little weasel Vice President of ours suggesting that we plant some dirt on Mr. Ramos?"

"Dirty politics seem to have no limits, especially when a political race is on the brink of defeat," Buttler answered without hesitation.

Bill changed the subject again, and declared, "I may be jeopardizing my job, but I'm going to go out and look for whoever is trying to assassinate Mr. Ramos. I cannot be cooped up in my office knowing that there is an assassin on the loose out there. I'll tell you this, I want to be the one that puts the handcuffs on this mysterious hitman before he draws a bead on Mr. Ramos or anybody else again. This may be my last chance, to do one more time, what has been in my blood since becoming a cop. You know, the thrill of the hunt, the excitement, and the danger. Hell, that is why I became a law enforcement officer in the first place." He was talking like a kid that wanted a new bicycle at any cost.

Tom did not say anything. He knew his friend, and it would not matter anyway. Bill was going to do whatever was in his mind no matter what. They rode in silence the rest of the way, each preoccupied with their own thoughts. That was their way.

CHAPTER 13

▼

Hans was out of his motel room in Montreal, Canada for the third and last time. He had carefully selected the site for the pigeon hunt. As he walked to his rented car, he talked to himself. "Now back to the motel room and wait. It wasn't comfortable walking on crutches when I didn't have to, but it made my disguise more realistic. There was no way to make this job a cakewalk, but none of the other jobs were either." The only thing that was going to make it easier was the fact that he had one more job to do, and then he was going to retire.

Before he opened the door to his motel room, Hans checked for a small piece of cellophane paper he had carefully inserted between the bottom of the door and the doorjamb. It was still there. Hans was a very cautious man. In this type of business you had to be—one small mistake and it was all over. It's the little things that the average man does not notice that makes the difference whether a man lives or dies. The years of training played an important part in Hans staying alive, but the instinct of survival that some people are born with, is what gave a man like Hans the edge.

✳   ✳   ✳   ✳

At the Sierra Club Headquarters in Carmel, California, the meeting was long and grueling, and still they had no definite answer. Club President, Paul Wessel, began to show some sign of disgust with the whole thing when he said that the mining industry was solidly behind the Third Party. "Ramos is the product of a small mining town and has hinted legislation to open Federal land to mining. Cattle ranchers are also backing the Third Party. By themselves, they are not big threat, but too many other groups are ready to endorse the Third Party also. We have a big problem. Our friends in Washington are beginning to panic. Let's get our heads together and come up with an answer, and remember that money will not be the answer this time."

Across the country in Chicago, American Federation of Labor President Harvey Fisher made sure that every union was represented at this very important meeting. In his speech, he reminded everybody that this Presidential election was the best chance the unions had to vote for a pro-labor President. He told them that the union movement was once again becoming strong. He reminded them how the union's high cycle revolves around the work force. He said, "If the work force is big, labor movement loses bargaining power. But when the work force is small, as it was during the World War II, then the unions are pretty much in the driver's seat. We don't want the unions in the driver's seat. All we ask for is a fair share of the jobs and to keep America strong. The Third Party has the right idea in trying to get industry, labor, and government to work together to reach a happy medium where there are no losers. Ramos also is looking to bring the factories back to our country in order for the American people to have the needed jobs."

Mr. Fisher did not have to remind them that in the last decade the American worker had suffered wage losses, benefits such as health insurance, cost of living raises, and job security, all because of greedy big business. But he also told them that the unions had their share of misconduct by letting hoods and gangsters infiltrate some top jobs in organized labor.

Before he finished he told them that every union had to work hard to help the Third Party in their bid for the presidency. "Every union member must vote and try to get their friends, neighbors and anybody they can convince to vote Third Party. Go out to the streets of the town, the state, the nation. Knock on doors. Talk to the people. Let them know the change the Third Party is willing to implement will benefit the whole nation." The last thing Harvey Fisher said was that the *America for Americans* slogan that Ramos was pushing, would favor the workers and not the special interest groups.

At the meeting of the California Mining Association in Sacramento, Association President, Mr. Phil McKanzie, spoke to the crowd. "Ladies and gentlemen, we all know why we are here. We haven't much time, so I'll make this short and sweet. Well, I'll just make it short."

"You all know that in the last decade, we have been losing ground in the fight to open new mines and keep old ones. Mining permits are getting scarce. You all know the reason for that. What is important now is the future of mining in

America. Whatever your present political preferences are must now be sacrificed for the sake of mining—your future. The only party that is willing to help the mining industry is the Third Party. It is imperative that we get behind the Third Party in order to survive. Ramos was born and raised in a mining town where generations of his family were miners, and he has promised to keep the mines open. We must not only vote for the man, we should also go to the mines and persuade the miners to vote for him."

"There is one more thing the Third Party is very much for—the pro-labor movement. I strongly believe that we can manipulate this wonder boy when we need to. That will be the easy part. Meeting adjourned."

CHAPTER 14

▼

Karlos was a good friend and instructor, and was very dedicated to his profession. He also treated Hans with honesty and respect. One day he surprised Hans and said, "Everything that I teach you to do will be exactly the way I do the jobs. There will be no deviation from the 'MO'. The reason for that is, whenever you do a job on a pigeon, I want the authorities to think it was me. I want them confused because they don't know you exist. When you finish the hunt in Montreal and the one in the United States, Interpol will be looking for me in that area, giving me a chance to move safer in Africa."

He continued, "There are two things that I want you to remember. One. Never accept a job directly face to face with the customer. Two. If you are on a pigeon hunt, do not carry anything that will identify you, or me for that matter. Good luck and good hunting."

So far, Karlos had planned all the jobs. One of his favorite tactics to make sure the job was done, was to use a decoy, or hawk, as he called it, whenever it was necessary. The hawk never knew Karlos existed and to Karlos, hawks were expendable. He arranged for a hawk to be used on Hans' last hunt. If the hawk eliminated the pigeon, he got one-half of the take. Getting caught or getting killed was no option; he would lose all the way.

Finding an apartment one mile away from the Third Party's headquarters in Baltimore was a stroke of luck for Kerns. Using the alias of Albert Jonen, the same name that was on his birth certificate, driver license and other phony papers that Karlos made up for him, he paid for three month's rent and moved in.

The place was a small cottage type building. At one time it had been a three-car garage and somebody had skillfully turned it into a mother-in-law quarters. The place was just as skillfully furnished and decorated. It was owned by an elderly lady who was on a fixed income and was renting it to supplement her retirement. The cottage was located about fifty feet from the main house and the front door of the apartment faced the alley. The door led to a carport that almost touched the three-foot block wall. All the houses along the alley had the same type of walls. The houses could hardly be seen because of the tall trees that grew past the high walls. Hans was lucky he could see most of the alley from the bedroom window that faced the alley. When he first saw the place, he was amazed at the privacy. All he needed now was a few groceries. He put his stuff away and decided to go to the store.

Going to the supermarket was an activity Hans had not done for a while. Since going AWOL from the army, most of his time had been spent in Algeria and other African countries. He had also done some pigeon hunting in the Middle East, Europe and South America. He wasn't a stranger to supermarkets but his lifestyle kept him away from that type of activity.

Kerns had been in the store about fifteen minutes when he noticed a tall man watching him. Being an extremely cautious man, Hans casually walked down three aisles to a magazine rack as if he was looking for something to read. He wanted to avoid the stares of the tall man. The man turned and moved on. *Nobody knows me here, so why am I so damn jumpy? That is contrary to my training.* When he saw the man limp out of the store, he finally relaxed. He paid for the groceries and walked out of the store.

Twenty minutes later, Hans was back in his apartment, half lying against the headboard of the bed. He opened up a can of beer, and watched some kids play in the alley. As he watched the kids, he began to think of his younger days. He never had a good childhood. He grew up hating people. He was a loner, and the only friend he had was Bruno, his younger brother. His family was poor, but his father always managed to have the money to drink. He remembered the beatings he and his sister got when his father came home drunk. As they grew a little older, it was his mother who took the beatings.

As he remembered, he talked to himself, and asked himself questions that had no answers. "Why was I always on the side of my father? I knew very well that what he was doing was wrong. I loved my mother but I could not get along with her. I wonder where she is now. I haven't seen her since I ran away from home. I really wish that things had been different. I understand now that I treated her bad, but I will make it up to her."

"I have one more job to do and that will be the last. I honestly hate what I am doing now, but it is the only thing I know how to do. When I'm done with this last job, I will go back to Arizona, I will buy my mother a new home, and I'll make sure she has all the things that she ever wanted." He kept talking as if he was in a trance. "I want to see my brother and sister. Hell, I don't even know what they look like now after all these years. I wonder if they remember me. God, I am sorry for what I have done, truly sorry. I hate what I have become, this loneliness. I am sorry God! I am so sorry!"

CLANG! The noise jolted him back to reality. He looked down at the floor, and realized where the noise came from. He had finished a twelve pack of beer, and the last half-empty can dropped from his hand as he daydreamed. Suddenly his face felt wet. He stood up, went to the mirror, and saw the tears in his eyes. He had been crying. He could not remember the last time he shed a tear.

He had no idea why he had cried. Whatever it was, he put it out of his mind. He pulled out a piece of paper from his shirt pocket. The note contained a telephone number and a short message which read, *important—call at exactly 8:00 p.m.* "That is tomorrow," he said to himself, and went to bed.

At 8:00 o'clock the next night, Hans stood in a phone booth three miles from his place. He picked up the receiver, dropped a quarter in the coin slot, and dialed a number. He had been anxiously waiting all day, thinking about this being his last hunt. A month ago, as he left Karlos' place in Algeria, Karlos talked to him for the last time. He explained that this would end their friendship forever. Hans had one more hunt in Montreal, Canada and one in the United States. The money from the last hunt in the United States, $250,000, would all go to Hans. His share from the one in Montreal would be $50,000. That money would be deposited in Hans' alias name of Kross Bunderbug's bank account in Zurich, Switzerland.

Karlos also reminded him that he was getting out of the business. He reasoned that age was creeping up on him, and that Interpol was dangerously close on his trail. That was enough incentive for Karlos to disappear from the face of the earth. He also advised him, for the last time, to hit your pigeon, cover your tracks, and disappear.

Karlos made all the arrangements and checked all the details, and Hans trusted him with his life. Karlos had a perfect way of doing business and as far as Hans knew, only one person had ever dared to cross him. That person's head was found in the middle of a street in Paris with his genitals stuffed in its mouth.

Yes, Hans was very cautious, but he felt safe. Hans heard the voice on the other end of the line say, "Pigeon hunter?"

He replied, "Depends on you favorite color."

The answer came back immediately, in a very deep voice, "White."

Hans hung up the receiver, waited for a moment in the phone booth, then opened the door and walked out.

That was all there was to it. The hunt was a go. From now on, come hell or high water, all his efforts would go towards the task ahead. As soon as he was inside his apartment, Hans removed the false leg cast he was wearing. Then he went to his suitcase and pulled out a large yellow envelope, and dropped the contents on the bed. He had to see the picture again. He had only seen it once after he was safely out of Canada and in a motel room in the United States. In his line of work, you couldn't have any other job on your mind until the one you were working on was finished. The rule was finish the job and get the hell out. Then you can think of other jobs.

Hans picked up a picture and looked at it for a long time. As he looked at the picture, his right hand went to his mouth, touching the solid gold front tooth. "Yes, I remember this man. He is the one responsible for this missing tooth," Hans mumbled. He dropped the picture and picked up another one. Hans smiled as he walked to the small kitchen. He opened the fridge door and pulled out a beer.

"Funny how things work out. The one person I promised myself to do away with many years ago, turns out to be a pigeon." Hans was talking to himself again. "Hell, this one would have gladly been a freebie." The one thing he could not comprehend was the fact that the pigeon was running for President of the United States.

Yes, he knew this man very well. In other hunts, faces and names did not matter. Names were a part of the face and not the other way around. The face of the pigeon was always the last thing the hunter saw seconds before he squeezed the trigger. Again Hans looked at the picture and asked himself, "Could this really be? Could this be the man that I promised to kill many years ago?" He looked at the picture one more time. "Yes, I forgot the name, but the face, never."

Hans continued to talk to himself. "What the hell is he thinking running for President of the United States? What a fucking joke, a damn greaser running for President. Only in America. So what if it is only the Third Party?" Hans was about to say something else on the subject when he remembered his sister. "My sister, Jenny, she couldn't be involved with that damn greaser, could she? No, my sister was smarter than that. As she got older she probably found out what greasers were and dumped him." Of that, Hans was certain.

"She was a Kerns, wasn't she?" He began to think of his last name. "How long had it been since I used that name?" Before he got too involved in distracting thoughts, Hans dropped the picture back in the envelope. He put the envelope in the suitcase, went to the small kitchen, and grabbed one of the crutches that leaned against the wall.

The crutch was in effect a rifle, very cleverly designed by a German gunsmith who was also a machinist. He made it look like a crutch, and it could be used as one. Any person who knew for the first time that the crutch was actually a rifle, would think that the rifle would have to have a very complex mechanism. In reality, it was very simple. The handgrip on the crutch had a small pin that when pressed, would pop up a 1¾ inch by ¾ inch crosshair scope. The small scope was pre-sighted to be accurate up to 100 meters. The scope was the brainchild of an employee at a camera factory in Wilsar, Germany where they produce some of the best cameras in the world. The optics were superb in brilliant luminosity, needle-sharp focus and of total chromatic correction.

Hans had never used it at the 100 meters distance. Most of his shots had been between 50 and 75 meters and he had always hit the bull's eye. As the scope popped up, a ½ inch trigger would drop down to his trigger finger, all in one motion. The other crutch had an adjustment to lower or raise the crutch by turning two wing nuts. On this particular crutch, one of the wing nuts was actually the firing pin. By pulling the wing nut back ½ inch, the gun was cocked ready to fire.

The receiver and barrel were made out of titanium, a very tough but very light metal. They were strategically located inside the tubular straight part of the crutch. The receiver was machined to accommodate a single 150-grain, .30-06 caliber round. Hans cleaned all the moving parts and made sure they worked. Finally, he applied a dab of gun oil from the small gun cleaning kit he carried in his suitcase. As he put the gun away, he told himself, "Tomorrow the greaser meets his maker, and the sooner I get this over with, the sooner I'll be ready to go home," and he went to sleep.

Early the next morning, after a shower and shave, Hans prepared breakfast. He was really excited, not because he enjoyed killing, but because this job would be his last. When he was a young boy in high school, he always wondered how it would feel to kill somebody. Then he shot the hobo in the railroad boxcar. He wasn't sure whether the man lived or died, and all this time he wondered with mixed emotions. One day he found the guts, and asked Karlos if there was any joy in killing people.

"It is not in the heart of most assassins to enjoy killing. It is just a well paid necessity and most of the time the pigeon needs to be disposed of," Karlos answered.

Thinking of what Karlos said, Hans remembered Johnson. Killing Johnson gave Hans satisfaction of revenge, not lust for blood. "He had it coming, damn nigger," Hans murmured.

After breakfast, he cleaned up the kitchen, and went to the small bedroom and began to pack. He had to be ready to move fast. As soon as the job was done, he intended to head for Arizona as soon as he could get out of the area. While he packed, Hans took special care not to leave any incriminating evidence in the small apartment. He removed the brown envelope and the tiny gun cleaning kit from the suitcase. He opened the envelope and took the picture and papers out. Hans looked at the picture for a moment. The he smiled and said, "Your time has come, Greaser."

As he tore the picture and papers into small pieces, Hans said, "How ironic, the only man I really hate in this world turns out to be my last hunt." Then he flushed the papers down the toilet. He finished around 11:00 A.M. He lay down on the couch and went to sleep. He needed all the rest he could get to have his mind clear for the task ahead.

CHAPTER 15

▼

George was in his study watching the news when the program was interrupted. The one thing that he never expected in his wildest dreams was showing on television. "None of that is true," he said. "There must be a mistake. There is no possible way that can be true. Is it possible they are so desperate that they can stoop so low in order to win an election? I know that mud slinging is a way of life in the political arena, but this is totally unacceptable. I'm an American citizen and this is my country." He felt utterly confused, so much so that he couldn't think. At times, it was anger and other times it was fear of the possibility that it could be true.

His wife and his son were also watching the news. Their eyes were glued to the television screen. "Those bastards!" Daniel yelled.

"Dan! That is no way to talk," his mother said, knowing that she felt the same way.

"But, Mother, don't you see what they are trying to do to Dad?"

"I understand very well but remember what your father taught you. Truth will prevail."

They both turned as they heard the door to the study open. George walked towards them, trying to hide his emotions, as he asked, "You saw that, huh?" They didn't say anything. George continued, "Pretty convincing story."

"Lies, all lies," Daniel said.

"Don't worry about it. It is a sign that they are getting desperate. If they can't prove it, the next thing they are going to be saying is that I'm an alien from Mars. Instead of pushing their agenda, discussing what is important to the voters, they just keep piling the dirt on. Remember that we have talked about this before and knew it was going to be rough."

"How do you counter something like that?" Daniel asked.

"I'm scheduled to go see my father tomorrow. He should give me what I need to put this nonsense to rest for good."

*   *   *   *

George recalled the telephone call he received from one of his brothers. His father had suffered another heart attack and was very ill. He quickly decided to fly to the Phoenix hospital where his father was. George knew he would have protection there, but he invited Mr. Perkins who agreed to go. Perkins met George's family and was very impressed with them. He thought that they were very polite, well mannered, and friendly. That night George's father took a turn for the worse. As was family tradition, the family took turns going in to talk to their father, the oldest first. George was the last one to go. As soon as he saw his father, George knew that the end was near.

George remembered the explanation his father gave him before he passed from this world. "George, I want you to understand that what happened when you were born was beyond my control. But not telling you, even though I wanted to tell you many times, was a bad decision, a mistake that I have regretted since you were born." There was a brief moment of silence. Then his father dropped the bomb.

"The fact is, you were born in Mexico." Before George could grasp the meaning of that last statement, his father continued, "You are not an American citizen."

"Who else knows?" George asked, his famous voice cracking.

"George, no one must know the truth."

"Who else knows this?" George asked as his voice become a bit more forceful.

"Just you and I."

His father looked very weak and his voice was beginning to fade a little. George sensed that his father needed to rest, and began to move away from the bed. He felt his father's hand on his wrist.

"Wait. You have to know how it happened. I don't have much time."

There was urgency in his weak voice, as he continued to say what must be said before it was too late. "Your mother and I were staying in Sonoyta just as we had done every weekday, while I was working in Mexico. The night your mother went into labor, we both made the mistake of thinking that it was the usual once-a-week pains she had been experiencing for a month. I remember that night very clearly because I have carried it right here all those years," he said, touching his heart. "The reason I could not tell you did not do anything to ease the pain."

He took a deep breath and then began to talk again. "That Tuesday night, about 11:30, her pains got unusually more severe than before. I decided to take your mother to Clarkston, which was about 140 miles from where we were. I knew that the border closed at 9:00 p.m. So I called John Lance, a very good friend of mine."

George's father met John in the Ironwood school many years ago. They played school sports together, graduated together, and became best of friends. He was the inspector on duty that night. "I told him the situation and that it was an emergency. He did not hesitate. He told me to come right on, and he would open the gate for me. He knew that I was taking a chance because of the distance, but after all, it was an emergency."

"We never made it. Her water broke and your mother was going to deliver in the car. I was desperately nervous and did not know what to do. Then, by chance, I saw a small house just off the road. I drove to the front yard, ran to the front door, and desperately began to knock. It seemed like an eternity, but no sooner than I started to knock, the door opened and a woman stepped out. Quickly I told her my problem."

"Bring her in the house," she said.

"A boy about 14 years old came out and gave me a hand. We took your mother into a small bedroom and laid her down on a brass frame bed." George was so taken with his father's story that he felt as if he was there watching every move.

"The woman ordered the boy to heat up some water on a wood stove in the kitchen. Then she handed me a clean bed sheet and told me to cut it up in small pieces. That woman knew exactly what to do. She was a 'Partera.' That is the Spanish word for midwife. I remember thinking somebody upstairs is looking after us." Tears rolled down his face, as his father continued.

"When I heard you cry and saw you for the first time, I thought that the ordeal was over. Then the woman motioned for me to follow her. When we were in the kitchen, she told me that your mother lost a lot of blood, was very weak and that I should take her to a hospital as soon as possible. I knew then that time was of the essence. The boy helped me carry your mom and laid her on the back seat. We put you in a wicker basket behind the passenger seat with blankets and a pillow we had brought from our place in town. Both of you were covered up real good. I tried to give the lady money but she would not accept it. I thanked her and drove out of there thinking, 'God help me get them to the hospital fast.' "When we arrived at the border, twenty-three miles from the place you were born, John was waiting by the open gate."

His dad stopped talking for a short moment. In his mind, George saw the border crossing which he had seen many times when he was a kid. The border crossing was not on the main highway, and used mostly by ranchers and Tohono O'odham Indians since it was close to the Indian reservation. Henry Ramos used it every week as he traveled to work in Mexico. It was convenient for him because he would cut the distance by twenty-five miles and the fact that his very good friend John Lance worked there.

"Now I will tell you what made it so difficult to explain all this to you. John was standing by the gate and did not look at the inside of the car. He asked how your mother was doing as he held the gate open for us. I told him that she was asleep now, but that she was very sick and needed to be at the hospital at once. I also told him that I needed to explain something first. John waved me by, and said, 'Get her to the hospital now and tell me later, just keep the opening of the gate to yourself. Now go!' Any delay in time and either one or both of you might not have made it to the hospital. I had to make a choice."

He continued with tears in his eyes, "When the time came for the paperwork, I had to tell the doctor that you were born in the back seat of the car on the way to the hospital. You have to understand that I could not tell them about John opening the gate at that time of the night. It was illegal and John could have lost his job. That is why your birth certificate indicates that you were born at Clarkston Hospital."

George tried to hold back his tears and asked his father, "What did Mr. Lance have to say when you told him about it?"

"That is another reason I have not told anybody, not even your brothers. I went to Sonoyta three days after you were born. All the way to the border, I was having a hell of a time thinking what I was going to say to John. When I stopped at the gate, I was surprised to see another officer there. I knew that John should be on duty. I asked the officer where John was, and he told me my friend had a massive heart attack that morning and was flown to Phoenix in critical condition. I thanked him and left. Later that night, I received a phone call from Phoenix. It was Kate, his wife. She told me that the heart attack caused too much damage to his heart and that he died."

"I was very saddened by his death. And the fact that I did not have a chance to tell him about the night's incident caused a feeling of guilt and shame in me. I felt as if I had stolen something from a very dear friend. I could not tell anybody. The damage was already done. Now I had to live with it."

"Two days before your mother died, I was sitting on her bed holding her hand when I felt her grab my wrist. Out of the blue sky she said, 'You haven't told him, have you?'"

"I looked at her and told her, 'I think he is still too young. Don't worry. I'll take care of it.' I will never forget the way she looked at me when she said, 'The longer you wait, the harder it's going to be for both of you.' After your mother passed on, I decided to tell you just as soon as you were old enough to understand, and many times, I wanted to do it. As the years went by, you turned out to be the perfect model of the All-American boy. That's what I thought anyway. By then, it was too late."

He waited for a moment, then continued, "I am sorry, Son. I know that was cowardly of me, but I just couldn't do it." By now, both were sobbing like two little kids. "Will you forgive me, Son? I know that I made a very bad mistake." He could barely get the words out.

"There is nothing to forgive. I know you tried." He was going to continue, but he would be talking to himself, for his father had passed away in his arms. George gently laid his father's head on the pillow, looked at him for a long time, then wiped the tears from his eyes and walked out of the room.

After the funeral, George and stayed behind at the cemetery to say goodbye to his parents. He buried his father right next to his mother, in accordance with his father's wish of many years ago. As George turned to go, he noticed a grave on the other side of his father's grave. The headstone read JOHN JACOBS LANCE. As he drove from the cemetery, George still thought of the irony of destiny. His father was now reunited in death with his best friend.

Later, when the family was back in Maryland, George had a hard time trying to hide his disappointment. He didn't say anything of what his father revealed to him. Jenny and Daniel noticed that George had been silent for a while. They didn't ask him anything. They knew that when the time was right, he would tell them. Finally, George spoke up.

"I have a crucial decision to make. What happened many years ago cannot be proved. It is all up to me. There are many things at stake here. But regardless of the outcome, I want you to be behind my decision and be proud of me." They did not understand what he was talking about, but they agreed.

"I'm going to schedule a press conference for later today. Right now, I have many things to do. I'll be in my study."

Later when George was preparing to go, Jenny asked, "Do you want us to go with you?"

"It is not necessary. This is something I have to do on my own."

On the way to the Third Party's headquarters, George stopped at St. Francis of Assisi Church for fifteen minutes. As he walked out of the church, he felt surprisingly calm. Now he could think clearly. He asked for guidance and believed he got it. When the limo stopped in front of the headquarters building, George felt good. As he got out of the car, he said to himself, "Showtime."

George knew there was no way out. In his entire life, he never had a more difficult decision to make. He had two choices. Choosing one way would make him champion of the Third Party, and turn him into the most powerful man in the world. It would also make his lifelong dream a reality, but would cost him his integrity and self-respect. It would make a farce of his campaign slogan *America for Americans*.

If he decided the other way, it would deprive the Third Party of a great victory, thus preventing them from making history by winning their first ever Presidential election. It would also take away the only chance he had to keep a promise he made to his mother many years ago.

The fame and honor his mother predicted for him the night she died may not ever materialize after today. Or would it? There was nobody left that could provide any information on what happened that night many years ago. But did it matter? He was the only one that knew. Even his brothers and sisters were not aware of it.

George was positive that in the end he would do the right thing. But what was the right thing to do? Who could ever believe that something that happened over fifty years ago would be the demise of his lifelong dream? Time was important. He would make his decision and act upon it today. Tomorrow would be too late.

CHAPTER 16

▼

Perkins talked on the phone from his office in Washington with Jackeau Levarne of the Canadian Interpol. "Are you sure it was Karlos?" Bill asked in disbelief.

"We don't have any hard facts, but the 'MO' fits Karlos to a T. We should know real soon though."

"Why is that?"

"Because as soon as the assassination happened in Montreal, the authorities threw a ten mile radius cordon around the place, and the Canadian border was sealed tight. Whoever he was will not get far," was the answer.

"Well, I wish you people all the luck in the world, because if it was Karlos, that son of a bitch is as slippery as an eel. We will keep an eye out for him."

A week later, Perkins had not heard anything from Canada. He decided to call Tom Buttler. They discussed the Montreal assassination, and Tom asked, "What do you think, Bill?

"To tell you the truth I have been worried all week long."

"You still think it was Karlos?"

"Yea," Perkins answered, looking down at the floor and nodding his head slowly.

Tom walked to the window then turned around to face Bill and said, "Let's look at it this way. The Canadians strongly believe it was Karlos because of the 'MO'. So if it were he doing that job first, and then coming here to shoot our man, he would be going against his own set of rules. Because you know as well as I do, he never does two jobs in less then eight months to a year. That is why he is so hard to catch."

"I know. But just think for a minute. He has been going at it for a long time. Don't you suppose that this late in the game he may want to change his ways—be more unpredictable in order to throw the authorities off his trail?"

"It is mind boggling, isn't it?" Bill said smiling.

"I don't want to change the subject, but Mr. Ramos called a press conference for tonight at 6:30. Are you set up for that?"

"Yes. It was a sudden change of schedule, but sure, I have three agents there."

"Good. I have two and there are security guards, but what bothers me is the press conference was announced on television and radio. There will be plenty of people there."

"I know," Tom answered. "When Ramos speaks, people listen."

"Yea, we better get going," Perkins said, as he grabbed his coat to leave.

The Third Party Headquarters was located across the street from a beautiful city park. The park had lots of trees, shrubs, and flowers. It also had a few gold-fish ponds and some heavy concrete benches. Distance marked walkways twisted and turned throughout the park.

A half-mile away from the park stood Johns Hopkins University. Hans figured that most of the traffic on that street was going to or from the University. He parked his car on Wolfe Street, somewhere between the University and Patterson Park, for two reasons. First, he wanted to study the escape route. Secondly, his car would blend in with the others from the University.

Hans picked the Third Party's headquarters for the final hunt. The building was exactly where the instructions said it would be. He was inside the building once, looking for a location to do the shooting. He decided he could do it inside the building, but it would be very risky. Karlos always said, "Risk is very much part of the job, but don't let risk dictate your plan of action. Remember that. You can be just as effective without being suicidal."

Hans knew he had to get within 75 to 100 yards of the target. He sat down on one of the park benches that faced the target area, and began to study the layout. The front of the building had a cement built podium to the right of the front entrance. It was located well away to the side, so if a band was playing or public speakers were doing their thing, people would not interfere as they went in and out of the building. There were a few places a man could hide and shoot from. If security were good, those would be the first places they would keep their eyes on.

Hans then spotted a hot dog vendor cart parked close to a four-foot block wall. The wall separated the headquarters building from a parking lot of the next building. Hans looked at his watch, and figured he had about a half hour before the pigeon began his press conference. He bought a hot dog and went to a huge rock that was next to the wall. There were three more of those rocks about the same size and all four were placed in a strategic location to give the landscape a look of age. As he sat on the rock and ate his hot dog, he thought of the three most important things to be aware of on a pigeon hunt: security, target distance, and escape route, not necessarily in that order. Security for high profile leaders and dignitaries is a critical issue these days. No one understood that better then the pigeon hunter.

It didn't take long for Hans to spot them. Four men and one woman were on the podium close to where the speaker would stand. One moved in between the crowd of newspaper people and photographers. The other two kept their eyes on the buildings north of the podium. *If that was all there was to their security, these guys need some advice from the Israeli police.* He figured that the distance from where he was at to the podium was about 80 yards, plus or minus a few feet. Karlos taught him how to use an object, any object close by, as an imaginary yardstick to estimate distances. He had never been off more than a foot and a half.

He saw the limo stop in front of the building in the horseshoe driveway and knew right away that the waiting was over. Hans watched as the pigeon and four other men got out of the big vehicle and walked up the steps to the podium. These men did not present a threat. They were all talking at the same time. *They have to be politicians.*

Hans was about to stand up when a big black car came to a screeching halt fifty feet from where he sat. The car was parked in a "No Parking Zone." Two men jumped out and began walking fast towards the podium. They came within thirty feet of Hans. As they were about to pass him, one of them turned his head for a short moment, and looked at the old man eating a hot dog. His companion had a radio in his left hand close to his ear. He grabbed his partner by the arm, and listened for a few seconds. He pointed to a building to the north of the podium, and then both headed in that direction. They walked as fast as they could without alarming the people there. Hans noticed that the man who turned to look his way was limping.

"Well, I'll be damned. That is the same man I saw at the supermarket. That son of a bitch is a bloodhound. He could make my job tougher," Hans quietly said to himself.

The sun was dipping in the southwest and the shadows were getting longer as the lights were turned on. Hans got in position by laying both crutches on top of the rock, and then leaned on the rock as if he was resting. Hans thought of how an easy pull on the small trigger would end another human life. The familiar sensation that came over him every time he was about to pull the trigger was present again, but with a difference. The ones before were routine, a job to be done. This one was payback time and he was going to enjoy it. Anyway, this was going to be his last one.

George exchanged a few friendly gestures to his supporters and people at the podium before he finally approached the microphone. Once he arrived at the speaker's podium, George stood straight and viewed the large crowd of supporters and media representatives that gathered before him. Cameras rolled, and flash bulbs popped everywhere. The usual smile was missing from George's face, but his charisma was present when he began to speak to the crowd.

"Ladies and gentlemen, as usual, I would like to ask all of you to help me recite the Pledge of Allegiance to the Flag." George was not wearing his coat. He wore a white shirt over the bulletproof vest. He faced the crowd and the American flag in front of him, and placed his right hand over his heart. He could feel the vest, but at that moment, he was not thinking of his safety. He felt his heart thumping through the vest, and that gave him the assurance that he was about to do the correct thing. He moved closer to the microphone. He glanced to the base of the microphone and mentally froze for a brief second as he observed the number twenty-three clearly marked.

"I pledge allegiance to the flag, of the United States of America, and to the Republic for which it stands, one nation under God," PLOP! Most of the people on the podium heard a noise like an ax hitting a soft log on the ground. At the same time, the ones that stood behind and to George's left were pelted with blood, flesh, and small pieces of skull bone. Then all hell broke loose as the screaming began.

"Oh, my God, he's been shot! Oh, God, somebody get ambulance! Get a doctor!" No doctor or ambulance would be of help to Mr. Ramos. He was dead before he hit the floor.

CHAPTER 17

▼

As soon as he pulled the trigger, Hans knew he had hit his target. The instant he saw the pigeon hit the ground he was on the move. He heard the screaming that came from the podium area, but he kept on going towards the park, moving as fast as he could without drawing any attention. When he reached the park, he stopped for a moment to reload, just in case. Before he moved again, he took one quick look to make sure no one was following him. Hans noticed people running in different directions, and saw, or thought he saw, a man moving towards the park and heading his way. He began to move again. As he walked, he thought out every move, and silently talked to himself, "Okay, Hans, here is where your training in evading goes into action."

William Perkins and Thomas Buttler quickly headed towards the podium area. They heard a call come over the radio that someone spotted a man with a rifle in one of the buildings a few yards away from the right side of the podium. As they changed directions and approached the site, plain clothes and uniformed officers converged all around the building. Tom flashed his badge, grabbed a uniform by the arm, and asked, "What have we got?"

"An armed individual has been cornered on the second floor. Two uniforms spotted him. They challenged him, and he shot and killed one of them. There are negotiations going on to get the man to surrender." Shots rang out before the officer could finish talking.

Somebody yelled, "They got him!" A moment later, "They are bringing him down on the elevator."

Tom got a good look at the subject and he determined two things. First, the obvious, the man was badly wounded. Second, he wasn't the man he had seen at the store. He walked back to where Bill stood taking notes. He looked Bill in the eyes and Bill understood what that look meant. The would-be assassin was the wrong man.

As they walked out of the building, Perkins remembered something that had been bothering him for a while. "That," he said, pointing his left thumb over his shoulder, "was the decoy that is referred to in Karlos' 'MO'. Nothing but a damned diversion." He didn't finish as they saw chaos in front of the podium. When they reached the podium, they sadly learned what had caused the chaos. Perkins saw the man he had learned to like and respect, dead on the podium. He clenched his teeth, and said, "Damn it!" then grabbed his radio.

Buttler got on his radio and screamed out orders. As he put his radio away, he turned his head in the direction of the hot dog cart and exclaimed, "Oh shit! Bill, come on!"

"Why, what's up?"

Tom motioned to Bill as he walked quickly in the direction of the stand, and explained, "When we went by here earlier, I saw a man that I thought looked familiar sitting on that rock." He pointed in the direction behind the cart.

"I was about to check him out, when we got that call about the would-be sniper."

"What did he look like?"

"He looked a lot like the man I saw at the supermarket, only older."

They looked at each other, and then Bill asked, "Are you thinking what I'm thinking?"

He nodded without saying anything.

At the cart, Tom asked the attendant, "Did you see a man on crutches go by here?"

"Yep," was the answer.

"Which way and how long ago?" Tom asked.

"The old man headed towards the park in that direction," the man said pointing with his left hand. "No more than two minutes, maybe." He then asked, "What's going on over there?" Neither one of them answered as they were on the move again.

They made a fast plan. Perkins would follow on foot and Buttler would take the car and try to get ahead of the subject, if he was still in the park. They couldn't afford to wait for backup because the shadows were getting longer and in ten to fifteen minutes, it would be too dark.

Perkins began to move fast. *This is my last chance. If that bastard is still in the park, his ass is mine.* He felt warm all over, and not because he was walking fast.

He felt the thrill of the hunt, like when a hunter's instinct tells him the prey is near and he is about to bag a trophy. Suddenly, he stopped. He realized too late that he had committed the cardinal sin when in pursuit. He had come around the slight bend too fast, and there was the man kneeling down, no more then thirty-five yards away, and pointing something in his direction. Perkins raised his gun but hesitated to pull the trigger for an instant. He saw that what was pointed at him was a mere crutch. His eyes widened as he tried to amend his mistake and pulled the trigger on the way to the ground.

Buttler heard one shot as he checked the outer edge of the park. He pulled his gun out and headed in the direction of the shot. It didn't take him long to find his friend. Perkins was on the ground mortally wounded. He managed to squeeze a round, but to no avail. Tom knelt close to his friend and tried to stop the bleeding. He whispered, "You are going to be okay. I have an ambulance coming."

Bill tried to say something, and Tom kept repeating, "Don't talk. You are going to be okay."

Perkins' voice weakened fast. Tom leaned close so he could hear what Perkins tried to say.

Perkins struggled to get the words out of his mouth. "Get him for me, buddy. Watch out for the crutch." They were the last words Perkins would ever speak. Tom cried silently and cradled Bill in his arms until the ambulance arrived.

Hans was sure that the man he just shot was one of the two men he saw earlier. "The bloodhound must be close by," he thought. He made it to his car without incident.

He noticed that the black car the men drove was parked about thirty feet from his car. Once in his car, he took off his false mustache, eyebrows, and cap. He also removed the false leg cast and the old coat, and he put a sweater on. He put everything into a plastic bag, and then headed west towards the scene of the crime. He figured that the search for him would be concentrated to the east in the direction of the seaports and airports. As he drove past the headquarters building, he saw that the place was crawling with people. He drove on, and when he came to a drive-in liquor store, he drove around the back, found a dumpster, and dropped the plastic bag in it.

Hans was willing to bet that the authorities thought that Karlos was responsible for the assassination. And if it was Karlos, he would be trying to get out of the country as soon as possible. In any case, whoever did it would not be going in the direction that he was going. He drove into Washington, DC. On the way out, he picked up a soldier that was thumbing a ride. The soldier was going to Albuquerque, New Mexico and that was fine with him. They would share the driving, thus moving faster out of the area. Also, it would look less suspicious with a soldier driving than a lone man would.

Hans highlighted his route on the map. From Baltimore he would head south-west to Nashville and Little Rock, then to Oklahoma City and Albuquerque. From there, he would head south to Las Cruces, New Mexico. At Las Cruces, he would go west to Tucson, Arizona and on to Clarkston, his hometown.

CHAPTER 18

▼

Jenny and her son were devastated. They watched the whole event happen on television. It wasn't long before Dector Jimenes and his wife came knocking at the Ramos' front door. Dector and George had become very close. The Jimenes family expressed their condolences, and offered to help in any way. Two of George's brothers and one sister flew to Baltimore to be with Jenny and her son Daniel. Jenny's younger brother, Bruno, a deputy sheriff in Clarkston, was also on the same flight.

The nation was stunned. Nobody wanted to believe that such a horrendous thing could happen again in this country. Some were sad, others were angry, but the majority wanted to know who and why, questions that at the moment had no answers. Talks of a conspiracy began to emerge. Why did this happen just before the election? Who was more than likely to profit from the assassination? More questions with no answers. Then there were whispers from people in the know, blaming a white supremacist group called The Order.

There were three men that were in some way connected with the assassination. One man knew or thought he knew who the assassin was and why he did it. Actually, he was half right. One was positive he had seen the face of the man who did the shooting, but could not say anything because he desperately needed a name to go with the face. The third man was the one that pulled the trigger, but he vanished without a trace as if the earth had swallowed him. The other two political parties openly denounced the assassination, but were secretly relieved of the threat of victory from the Third Party. The whole country was sad and grieved for a good man they had come to know and love.

Bruno was amazed at the number of people that kept arriving to express their condolences. He met many dignitaries, but one person he found very interesting was Tom Buttler. They talked about the assassination, and Bruno asked Tom, "Are there any good leads?"

"As you well know, in these types of cases, leads are few and far apart. But no matter how small or insignificant they are, we will follow them, and eventually we'll nab the guilty person. But, we do have this." Tom went to his inside coat pocket, pulled out a picture, and passed it to Bruno.

"Which one?" Bruno asked when he saw two men in the picture.

"If you notice, they both look alike. According the French Interpol, this one here," he said, pointing to one of the men in the picture, "is Karlos the Jackal." Then he asked, "Are you familiar with that name?"

Bruno nodded as looked at the picture. "Don't tell me he is the one?"

"Some people seem to think so. I don't. I believe it's the other one. Take a good look at it. He is supposed to be an American."

Bruno grabbed his chin in a deep thought, turned his head and looked away, and then came back to the picture. Tom noticed his peculiar behavior and asked, "You've seen this guy?"

"I don't believe so, but for some reason he reminds me of somebody. I just don't know who."

"He couldn't possibly have seen this man," Tom thought, "but he is just like any other young cop. I was the same when I first became an officer of the law. As a young cop one is always thinking of making that big collar, catching the big fish."

The conversation lead to Bruno's finishing his law enforcement training, as Tom said, "When you finish school, give me a call." He handed Bruno his business card.

A week before the assassination, the Secretary of the Army received Medina's documentation in the request for the Medal of Honor for Captain George Ramos. The Secretary was advised from his superiors that the presentation ceremony could wait until after the election. The President's schedule did not permit it until then.

All the way home, Bruno kept thinking of the man in the picture Buttler gave him. He felt certain he had seen that face before. *But was it possible?* His family moved from Alabama when he was very little, so he didn't remember much from that time. The other place he had been to was the Police Academy in Tucson, Arizona, but he could almost rule that out.

Without making any connection to the picture, Bruno began to think of his brother Hanson as he did almost every day. For Bruno, his big brother was his hero. Hanson used to take him rifle shooting out in the desert. At night, before they went to sleep, Hanson would read to him or tell him stories. He would also tell Bruno that they were best of friends and would always be best of friends. Bruno couldn't understand why Hanson had to leave. One thing Bruno was sure of, Hanson would return one day and would be very proud of him as a deputy sheriff.

Hans was coming from Tucson two days before the funeral. According to radio news, there were many dignitaries scheduled to attend the funeral. Hans was well aware that there would be a lot of law enforcement presence, including Secret Service and FBI agents. He had to be very careful. He figured to get a hotel room and stay out of the public eye for a while. He drove through the Tohono O'odham Indian Reservation, and enjoyed the drive's desert scenery. He had lived in the southwest desert a big part of his life and loved the desert.

Hans noticed an Indian Police cruiser about 100 yards behind him and that made him a little nervous. The Indian cop followed him until Hans crossed the reservation borderline and into Pima County. Hans looked in the rear view mirror and noticed that the cop stopped short of the reservation line and drove into a clearing off the highway. Hanson knew now that he was within a few miles of Clarkston. What he didn't know was that that he had made a small mistake. Somewhere between Maryland and Arizona, he was supposed to change the license plate on the car. He didn't want to change them while the soldier was with him. But after he dropped the soldier off in Albuquerque, New Mexico, he totally forgot. Changing the license plate was not critical, but it was a precaution.

"Breaker, breaker for Beetle Bug, you got a copy?

"Red Feather One to Beetle Bug, you got a copy? Red Feather One to Beetle Bug, you got a copy?"

"This is the one and only Beetle Bug. What it is, good buddy? Come on back."

"What's your 10-20? Come on."

"I'm returning from the Mexican border and I'm about one mile from the Tucson—Rocky Point junction. Come back"

"Wait at the J. You got a boggy coming your way. Wrong license plate. Like Maryland. Come on."

"Will check. Many, many, good buddy. Catch you on the rebound. Beetle Bug out."

Bruno and Mitch Santos, a reservation police officer, had CB radios installed in their cruisers at their own expense. It kept them awake on the graveyard shift. As he waited, Bruno thought about his CB handle. His brother gave it to him. Actually, the name his brother gave him was Stink Bug. Hans told Bruno that when Bruno was a baby and began crawling, he would raise his butt like a stink-bug. He smiled as he thought about that and almost missed the car as it went by. Bruno began to follow the car from a short distance. Sure enough, the car had a Maryland license plate but nothing else out of the ordinary.

Mitch had a hunch and Bruno trusted Mitch's instincts, but he needed a reason to stop the car and talk to the driver. Bruno was about to stop the car regardless of reason, when the car ahead of him signaled a left turn off the highway onto Darby Well Road.

Hans wanted to know if the cop was just trying to get on his nerves or if it was something more serious. Off the highway was a big area for parking off Darby Well Road and Hans turned into it. By the time officer Kerns arrived at the parking area, Hans was out of the car with his weight on the crutches and leaning against the car door. Bruno wasn't worried, it was just a routine check. *No big deal.* He parked about ten feet from the other car, got out of the cruiser and slowly walked towards it, thinking of what to say.

"Howdy. I stopped to see if you have a problem or need help."

"No, there is no problem. Just stopped for a little rest. Long drive, you know."

They looked at each other no more than five feet apart. Bruno saw the face and knew instantly he was looking at the face of the man in the picture. This one had a small mustache and made him look a little older, but it was him. He remembered Tom telling him about the crutches, and he knew right away he had walked into a trap.

I have to keep talking to get the drop on him. He and Mitch had practiced a move numerous times while they were off duty. *The time has come. This is no dry run.*

"You have a good day, Sir," he said, as he walked back to his car. "This front tire has something stuck on it. It's making a funny noise," he said, as he bent down to look at the tire. He turned his body a little to hide his hand as he grabbed his pistol. What he didn't count on was that the man he figured to get the drop on was a master at this kind of stuff. As Bruno moved up with gun in hand, he saw the other man had the right crutch at waist level and was swinging in his direction. In a fraction of a second, Bruno twisted his body left and pulled the trigger. He felt as if a heavy object hit him in the chest and knocked him down to the ground. After a moment that seemed like hours, Bruno looked at the

94 First Mexican

subject and saw that he was also hit, but he was still alive. The crutch lay on the ground about three feet away from the subject. Bruno checked himself quickly and saw that he was bleeding heavily from the left upper chest and under the left arm.

Bruno hurt badly, but he managed to get up slowly and walk over to the man who sat on the ground with his back resting against the car door. Bruno saw the man was badly wounded in the upper chest and blood flowed out of his mouth. Bruno was just a few feet away when the man looked up and saw the nametag above Bruno's shirt pocket. His eyes widened as he read the tag, OFFICER BRUNO KERNS. He blew some blood out of his mouth and softly said, "Stink Bug?"

Bruno heard him and yelled, "What did you say?

"Stink bug," he repeated.

"Who the hell are you?" Bruno asked.

"I'm your brother, Hanson, your best friend, remember?" His voice was getting weaker.

"Oh my God nooooo," Bruno yelled, as he heard a car stop nearby. It was Mitch. "Get an ambulance. Hurry!"

"It's on the way. I called when I saw you guys on the ground."

Bruno could not believe what had happened. What he was sure of was that Hans was the only person in the world that knew his nickname. He put his arms around Hans and cried, "Why, Hans, why?"

Hans just looked at him with tears in his eyes and said, "Tell Mother I love her, and you are still my best friend." He turned his head to the side and died.

Mitch was worried about Bruno's condition but he didn't want to interfere. Bruno released Hans and weakly stood up as Mitch asked, "What's going on, bro?"

Bruno took a short step, looked at his right hand, and saw that he still had his pistol. He yelled like a crazy man and threw his gun against his cruiser.

"What the hell is going on, bro?" Mitch asked, this time very concerned.

"I just killed my own brother, damn it!" He turned and tried to run and fell flat on his face.

A helicopter flew Bruno to a Phoenix hospital where the doctors declared him a very lucky man. The bullet hit him on one of his upper ribs and was deflected to the outside, opening a three-inch hole close to the armpit. It also tore a chunk of flesh inside his left arm. That was the good news. The doctors found that Bruno had been through a very traumatic experience. The emotional shock left him speechless and in a trance. The doctors told Bruno's mother not to worry. With therapy, in two or three months he would be as good as new.

CHAPTER 19

▼

On his way home, Senator Graves stopped at a liquor store to buy a bottle of Schnapps. He smiled, thrilled that white America had dodged a bullet. A leading Presidential candidate had taken one in the head and the incumbent President would serve for four more years. The Senator figured that things were moving according to his plans.

Now he was ready. He had been planning to run for President for a few years, but he knew that he had to be patient and slowly follow his well-laid plans. The hardest part of his plan, he thought, was to unite the white supremacist groups to work together instead of against each other. Many of them were gaining political offices and many others were infiltrating law enforcement agencies all over the nation, giving the Senator a brazen attitude. "Yes," he said, "time is on my side. Four years from now, when I become President, then the rescue of America from the fires of racial degradation for the sake of our nation's destiny will began." That was his warped belief.

Senator Graves was so preoccupied with his thoughts of the future that he neglected to notice a dark figure that noiselessly moved behind him. As he reached with the car keys to open the door, he felt an object press against his back and heard the words, "Don't turn around, Mister!"

"What the fu…" He didn't finish.

"Mister, I have a .45 caliber pistol on your back. If you turn around or make one unnecessary move, you are a dead moddafucker."

"What the hell do you want from me?" The Senator was angry.

"This may sound crazy to you, but all I want is enough for a meal and a birth-day present for my boy."

"Do you have any idea who you are talking to?" The Senator tried to impress the man with the gun as he had done with his colleagues, always believing he was superior to others.

"Mister, I don't give a shit if you are the President of the United States. All I want is your wallet. I'll take what I need and then hand it back to you. Then you can go home and thank the Lord you will see another Christmas," The gunman had a deep frog-like voice.

The Senator was now past the boiling point of his rage, but in the twisted warped mind of his super ego, he managed a smile, thinking, "Mister, four years from now, you would have hit the nail on the head." He came back to his senses as he heard the voice.

"Now give me the wallet."

"I'll show you who you are dealing with, you son of a bitch!" the Senator yelled. He then turned around, making a fatal sudden move with his right hand to his left inside coat packet. The gunman reacted, not with malice, but on the instinct of survival that the United States Marine Corps deeply instilled in him, before they sent him to Korea. The nearby traffic muted the blast of the gun. The Senator saw the flash of the gun barrel. At the same moment, he felt as if something pushed him, and his body slammed against his car. The .45 caliber slug that hit him in the chest tore through ribs, cartilage, one half of his heart, part of his lungs, and exited below the left shoulder blade, leaving a four-inch gaping hole in his back.

The Senator had a surprised look on his face at first. Then, as he slid down the side of his car, the last facial expression the Senator would ever have was that of intense hate and rage. He looked up at the black man holding the smoking gun, and the Senator died an angry man, as his eyes sent false testament of his beliefs to his warped mind. Then his right hand opened up, showing a card.

The black man knelt down, slipped his hand in the Senator's coat pocket, and pulled out a wallet. He rifled through some bills, pulled out two one hundred dollar bills, and returned the wallet to its place. He was about to stand up when he looked at the business card in the Senator's hand, and curiously picked it up. He stood up over the Senator's body and read it in the dim light, *Senator Karl Graves*, in large letters. Below the Senator's name were smaller letters he could hardly see which read, *Proud To Be a Real American.*

The black man looked at the dead man for an instant, flipped the card on the dead man's chest, and walked into the night.

Two hours later, the police responded to a call of a dead man behind a liquor store. When they identified the subject as a United States Senator, the FBI took over the case. The FBI found out that the Senator was well known to the people working at the liquor store. He would stop and buy a bottle of Schnapps about every two weeks. His two gold rings, a very expensive watch, his money, and all his credit cards were still in his possession.

At first, a random robbery was ruled out. Senator Graves had been a single man all his life. He lived with his mother in a big house in Virginia, but he also had an apartment in Washington. When the FBI went to his apartment to look for clues in his death, they found more then they had bargained for.

They found very specific plans as to how he was going to become President of the United States. After becoming President, he would turn this country into an all white nation and eventually into a totalitarian state with him as absolute ruler. Other plans included building the most powerful military force in the world, invading Mexico, and convincing Canada to join him in dominating the world. There was a journal explaining how Hitler almost got it done. The problem was that Hitler was stubborn, arrogant, and not too smart, or he would have done it. In the journal, there was also information implicating the incumbent President in the assassination of the Third Party's candidate. There were also tape recordings of top members of the administration making shadowy deals with big business and other shenanigans that would be very embarrassing to the administration if the information were made public.

The FBI agents also found some more papers. Carefully hidden in the lining of the journal were two birth certificates. One was on yellowed parchment, written in German. The other was a fake certificate that documented Graves' birthplace as Sacramento, California. Graves did not plan to let something so minor as the United States Constitution keep him from becoming President.

The FBI decided that the Senator was a complete idiot or just totally crazy. In any case, the information found would be tightly sealed from the media and public. They declared the Senator's death was a robbery/homicide. The FBI took a big chance by not making what they found public, but it was all in the interest of the nation. By making it public, even though some of the information could not be verified, it could possibly bring the government to its knees, and this wasn't the time for a scandal.

*   *   *   *

When Buttler heard of the killing in Arizona, he immediately went to Clarkston for verification. He stayed in Phoenix long enough to go to the hospital to check on Bruno. He did not have a chance to talk to him because of Bruno's condition. As he stood there looking at Bruno, he thought, "You did good, kid. You beat me to him. I hope that what happened will not ruin your life. When you get out of the hospital it will be hard for you to face it. It will be another chapter in your life and you have to grow with it. What happened wasn't your fault. It was meant to be."

Buttler remembered what happened to his best friend. He continued, "Your destiny was determined long ago." With that he walked out of the room. Before he left Phoenix he told Bruno's mother what to expect when Bruno leaves the hospital. He left his card with her, and told her that if she needed any help in the future, to call him.

Buttler was opposed to the lid placed on the findings regarding the Senator's death. He understood that it had been a hard decision to make by his superiors. But right or wrong, he didn't want any part of it. He decided that it was time to go fishing, and without any fanfare, he retired.

∗   ∗   ∗   ∗

There were hundreds upon hundreds of people at the small cemetery on the day of the funeral. The majority of the people in Clarkston had never seen a limousine in their entire life. The people of Clarkston were stunned by the long line of limos that brought dignitaries from all over the country.

At the entrance to the cemetery, two men stood with a pickup truck full of small American flags. Nobody knew who was responsible for the flags, but the two men passed the flags out to everyone as they entered the cemetery. A few people thought that what they were seeing was odd, but most of them knew that the flags gave the occasion a profound meaning.

Attending the funeral was a color guard from Fort Ord, California. There was a platoon of Rangers in full battle dress from the same company that George had served with in Vietnam. The Rangers volunteered to carry their fallen friend from church to the cemetery, taking turns carrying the casket six men at a time. Six veterans that had served with George in Korea, now served as pallbearers.

After *Taps*, the formation of the missing man flew over the cemetery. Then a group from Maryland sang *America the Beautiful*. After the folded American flag was presented to Jenny, the Secretary of the Army did something that was unheard of before. Posthumously, presentation of the Medal of Honor is usually done only by the President, in a ceremony in Washington, DC. Nobody was prepared for what unfolded there. In the shortest and most unusual ceremony on record, the Secretary presented Jenny with George's Medal of Honor. The Secretary knew that after what he had done, his job was in jeopardy, but he did not care. When he was told that the presentation of the medal would have to wait until after the election, he figured that it was being done for political reasons. He decided to do it on his own, even though he knew his job was on the line. Then the assassination happened and that made his decision easier.

When the military service ended, Daniel Ramos stood up, walked to the casket, and began to speak. "My father was a man of integrity. Good. Loving. And of excellent character. He believed in people, and had an ardent love for his country. A few weeks ago, I noticed a change in him. I believe now that he had a premonition that something was going to happen to him. He called me into his study and we talked for a long time. He told me many things about life that he had never talked about before. A lot of what he told me was about his life. The things that impressed me the most was the story of him and his childhood friend, Eddie. The one thing they both wanted to take with them to their graves was the American flag. The other thing was that the rule of life was to be born and to die. He said that it was what you did in between that was responsible for the legacy you leave in this world. He also told me not to be afraid to daydream. If a man accomplishes his dream, he can dictate his own destiny, and in the process, change the course of history. The last thing he told me was that not all dreamers become great but that all great men were once dreamers. I didn't say anything then but I will say this now," he continued, as he turned towards the casket.

"In your field of dreams you sowed a small American flag, keeping a promise you made to a childhood best friend. You cultivated it with honesty, compassion, courage, and love for country. This is your harvest." He extended his arm and turned a full 360 degrees. "You managed to unite a nation that was desperately in a need of unification. We know that your body will not lay in wake at the Capitol Rotunda, that you will not be buried at the Arlington Cemetery. But to your family and to most of the people of in this country, in your legacy, you will be remembered as the President that never was."

"My father was a man on a mission. He was going to accomplish a dream and deliver on a promise he had made to his dying mother. He lit the torch of dreams and was well on his way, but his journey was cut short by an assassin's bullet." Daniel paused for a moment then he continued.

"Now hear me good. I will pick up the torch and carry it. If I don't make it, the next generation will carry it, and the next, until the torch gets to its intended destination. This is a promise. Now, please, help me recite the Pledge of Allegiance for my father's last time."

After a moment of silence, they all began.

"I pledge allegiance to the flag of the United States of America and to the republic for which it stands, one nation under God." As he said that, Daniel looked up towards the mountain. He saw the big cross on the mountain, and the flag at the cemetery below the cross gently waving with the wind.

First Mexicans

Dr. Ellen Ochoa—First Mexican-American female astronaut.

Richard Valens—First Mexican-American Rock Star.

David Barkley—First Mexican-American awarded the Medal of Honor.

Henry G. Cisneros—First Mexican-American mayor of a prominent American city (San Antonio) and member of President Clinton's cabinet.

Federico Pena—First Mexican-American to head the Department of Transportation.

Nancy Lopez—First Mexican-American female professional golfer inducted into the LPGA Hall of Fame.

Raul Castro—First Mexican-American governor of Arizona.

Anthony Muniz—First Mexican-American inducted in the Professional Football Hall of Fame.

Ed Pastor—First Mexican-American elected to Congress.

Linda Chavez-Thompson—First Mexican-American to serve on the executive council of the AFL-CIO.

Hector G. Godinez—First Mexican-American postmaster in the United States. (appointed by President John F. Kennedy)

Reynaldo Guerra Garza—First Mexican-American Federal District Court Judge in the United States. In 1979 Jimmy Carter appoints Judge Garza as the first Mexican-American to serve in the Fifth Circuit Court of Appeals.

Source: Library of Congress

978-0-595-36758-0

0-595-36758-5